CATHERWOOD

CATHERWOOD

Marly Youmans

LARGE PRINT BOOK CLUB EDITION

Farrar, Straus and Giroux
New York

This Large Print Edition, prepared especially for Doubleday Direct, Inc., contains the complete unabridged text of the original Publisher's Edition.

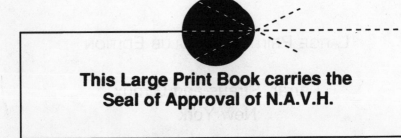

**This Large Print Book carries the
Seal of Approval of N.A.V.H.**

For Nancy Potts Coward

Contents

1676

1678

CONTENTS

1678

A Rainbow for Crows

1676

The Salt Seas

As the tide began to ebb, the ship's cannon fired, skeins of white smoke unreeling into the brisk March air. An answering cloud of smoke from shore tumbled across the crowd on the docks. At the ship's rail, Cath gripped Gabriel's arm, a cold wind dashing the tears from her eyes.

"Farewell, Lacey and Jamie!" Catherwood called.

The wind poured past the ship, hurling her words toward St. George's Channel and Cornwall, then on into wide spaces of ocean. Jamie rode high on Lacey's shoulders, waving a tin horn tied with ribbons, blowing on it to attract Cath's attention, although from so far she could hear nothing, the piping drowned in the weeping and cries of the other passengers. St. George's cross, scarlet as bloodstains on a field of snow, reared up the mast, rippling noisily as if it too would be hurtled toward the sea. The great sails, streaked and faded with salt, caught the wind with a series of sharp retorts, and the bluff-bowed ship rocked forward, bound for the Atlantic Ocean and the far country of Virginia.

"A sad beginning," said Gabriel. With Gabriel and Catherwood Lyte stood their own small family of servants, along with two de Bruton families, cousins to Gabriel. Standing and seated about them on deck were several hundred passengers, mostly boys and young men bound to Virginia as servants, many of them having been spirited from their homes by strangers. There were thirty-seven girls and women, one bartered away by her own husband, several transported for petty crimes or trepanned and sold for servants against their wills.

"Thank God ours is otherwise," said Cath. She knew her fortune might have been the same as theirs if Lacey's mother had not adopted her. The lot of such women would be very different from her own case, safely married with a dowry, tied to those whose Church of England relatives had migrated to Virginia decades before. The moment her adopted mother died, the way was determined for her, a busy, crowded route; after the funeral she would have to marry—after a hasty period of mourning, after banns, but before the prohibited time of Lent began. Now the months ahead of her lay like a great emptiness but one secure in its end, for the de Bruton and Lyte families would find in Virginia connections from England, friends of their parents and grandparents.

On the first night out she dreamed about the selling—her earliest memory.

As she staggered with the effort to keep up with the older children, Catherwood's bare feet pounded against the frosty ground, her inarticulate cries lost among their shouts. When one of the boys lurched and fell full length on the hard rutted road, the others laughed and raced on behind the carriage. Its wheels were big, spinning and slowing and spinning again, canary-yellow tops twinkling in a low landscape of mud and ice and hacked trees.

The older children jumped under a pelting rain of copper from the carriage, snatching at the air, scrambling perilously close to the elegant wheels. A blond head popped out of the carriage, the head of a man so bright and mischievous that he seemed barely more than a boy, though already twenty, hanging dangerously out of a carriage window, so far that his doublet of black camlet and costly blue scarf were visible, and all to toss a coin straight to the child who stumbled in the wake of the others. There was the sudden happy surprise of the coin skimming toward her, touching her lightly and pattering on the cold ground. A panicky voice that must have been her own cried *Mine, mine*.

Then she was in a one-room cave floored with packed dirt, with a stench of smoke and urine, and somewhere close by a pig rooting after a fistful of cold pottage dropped by a child. The gentleman and his lady cousins stood in lofty outlines against the doorway, the young ladies in their plush-lined cloaks holding handkerchiefs to their faces, then retreating back to the carriage. The children poured through the room, around the rocky shapes of two old women, a slumbering hog, a lame man. There was nothing like a mother in that memory, nothing. When the crooked man dragged Catherwood's shift up past her waist, showing her naked mound with its small cleft and her thin belly, she growled deep in her throat. Several gold coins, perfect, gleamed in the young man's sky-colored gloves.

She woke, her face wet, to see her husband's face close to her own. For an instant she was nameless and motherless—an unwashed child, hair beaded with nits—a girl sold to Lacey Grevel as a gift to his mother. Then lantern light threw its gold on the bed, on Gabriel's face. Catherwood shook her head, a tear rolling down the slope of her cheek.

"I dreamed about my brother."

The remainder of her story Cath could easily recite, for the servants at Grevel House never tired of telling the tale, as though it were a fairy story of a child of their own snatched up and set like a gift among the gentry. Mother Childe was fetched to douse her with the medicinal potions Cath recalled as both sweet- and evil-smelling, applying agrimony in grease to the ugly scab on her back, soaking her hair and scalp in vinegar and powdered lousewort seeds before patiently sliding the killed nits from her curly threads of hair.

Scrubbed clean, dressed in one of Lacey's yellowed baby gowns, she was presented to Mrs. Grevel. Elisabeth Grevel, although still angry with her son, examined the child carefully, then lifted her up.

Mrs. Grevel had given birth to three daughters in the years between Lacey's birth and the death of her husband at Edgehill early in the English Civil War. The second of these, Anne Catherwood Grevel, was stillborn; the eldest, Mary Catherwood Grevel, and youngest, Anne Catherine Grevel, along with their maternal grandmother and two servants, died in the space of three days during a brief outbreak of plague. Lacey, thinking to replace the loss of these little daughters in his mother's heart, carried the nameless child home. But Mrs. Grevel insisted that they search for the child's parents.

"We do not buy children. It is centuries since men and women of southern England were slaves on the great manors." Mrs. Grevel grasped her son's arm. "I know that human beings can still be sold in the countryside, but that don't make the practice agreeable to English Christians."

The son spent several penitential days riding out in the carriage. It was as though Lacey had snatched a child from the fairies, so little luck did they have discovering anyone to claim Cath. Having been thoughtless, impulsive, he could remember no more than that the cot-house stood close to a road, and he and his young cousins had spent the afternoon rattling about on lanes cobbled with fill and tracks barely passable to a carriage. William the coachman, who claimed to have been minding his own business, and the cousins, who barely knew the roads to their own door, were of even less help.

Wild and untaught, the child delighted both mother and son. For a long time, everything in her new world appeared wonderful to Catherwood. Sometimes she spent quiet minutes in her new mother's lap; sometimes she laughed uncontrollably at Lacey's tricks and silly faces; sometimes she dropped into fits of sobbing, murmuring words that Mrs. Grevel could make no sense of.

For many years she seemed a creature of the woods and meadows. She was pleased by the coarsest food; indifferent to summer's heat or autumn's cold, she would sometimes fall asleep while playing, to be carried home from the fields or garden. She hated wearing shoes, bathing, and sitting still at church. But as the years passed, Catherwood at last began to grow more and more like her adoptive mother, her early wildness almost lost in the study of proper manners and speech, needlework, the keeping of a country house.

The smell of the sea grew in intensity as the last glimpse of Ireland fell into the mist. The rich odor of the Irish coast, a fragrance of turf smoke and soil, dropped away. On the fifth day a dove lighted in the rigging, clinging there most of the afternoon.

"Lost," Henry Pasturel said, "traipsing about the seas."

"Months may pass before we see another," Gabriel Lyte said as the bird rose, buffeted back by the wind, then flew eastward toward Ireland.

"Fly home, sweetheart," Henry called. His brother, Will, slapped him on the back, telling him to hush, calling him a macky-moon.

The little family huddled at the rail, watching until the bird, mounting higher on the wind, vanished entirely. Fortune was with them, so far, the Lytes and their three servants proving good sailors, while the de Brutons confined themselves to their shared cabin, refusing even so much as pennyroyal, good against seasickness. Meanwhile Cath and Gabriel played at cards in their small cabin, ate as guests of Captain Chidgley, and lay in bed together so late that their men would have breakfasted, rolled up the wool bed by the door, and gone to take the air on deck before the two rose.

"I must be a sailor's child," Catherwood suggested.

"Not like my cousins," Gabriel said, burying his face in the curve of her neck, in her hair. "Green as the sea grasses.

"But my own father is a churchman, not a sailor," he added, rolling over on his back.

"Fisher of men," Cath said. "Thereby sailor, and thereby Gabriel Lyte is a sailor's child."

"Ah," said Gabriel, rifling through the bedclothes until he found his wife's smooth thighs. "Dear heart," he whispered, remembering an old poem, "how like you this?"

* * *

One evening Captain Chidgley called the Lytes to witness a small storm.

"Harmless," he promised, "and a rare sight."

The sky pinkened, and a dark cloak streaked with yellow widened over the horizon. The sailors scrambled to shorten sail, shouting back and forth in the rigging. A sudden forceful gust, a light, dry crack of lightning, and the cloud gathered the gloaming to itself, the sky around turning a pale and sickly yellow: then a lull, and the darkness contracted further. The moon, seeming to leap backward from a flotilla of small streaming clouds, fled behind the deep velvet. The ship burst forward as the dark split open, spilling its white seed like a magic trick, showering down countless small moons that rattled and shot from the masts and yards, bouncing and rolling across the deck, lodging in ringbolts and crevices. Sheltered under piled canvas, feeling the waxen stones pelt the heavy cloth, Catherwood and Gabriel pressed together, watching as the hail stopped as suddenly as it had begun. The winds tore a rift in the cloud, so that the moon gleamed out, ringed by a moonbow.

Day after day, the sky and sea paraded with infinite variety, from dull and leaden sea swelling slowly under a sky the color of a dove's wing to green whitecapped towers under sunshine, the air prismatic with suspended drops. The ship itself seemed a shapeshifter, drab sails hanging slack at one moment, at another appearing to shine white as snow hills, puffed up with the glittering salt air.

One morning, leaning over the rail, Cath pointed to a strange sad-colored creature that looked quizzically up at them, twisting its head to one side. There were other sights as strange: a winged fish that skipped on top of the water; a luminous, uncoiling creature, perhaps a great eel or a sea dragon; scattered wings of phosphorus that set the sea surface glimmering, leaving a shining wake behind the ship.

On the forty-second day out of Bristol, a boy of eleven died in steerage. Taken suddenly with trembling and a high fever, John Bird died after twelve hours, with his head in the lap of Mary Silverthorne, the woman who had been sold into service by her husband. The low mourning of the passengers, with now and then the high wail of a woman, could be heard throughout the ship, even by sailors who crept high into the rigging. John Bird had been homesick, longing for his mother, and Mary Silverthorne had set herself to be a second mother to him. She told Catherwood that he didn't want to go to Virginia, had been stolen away from his family and sold while on a journey to Bristol. Now he would never see Virginia; now he was safe from the hard life of the plantations. But Mary Silverthorne was not comforted, as John Bird had been a lively, kind boy who hoped to live out his service and return home again to Dorset. She knew all about the boy. His parents kept an inn at Melcombe Regis, and though the town was shabby and no longer the busy wool staple of earlier years, St. Mary Street had still been the best place in England to John Bird.

Even Captain Chidgley was a little shaken by the first death of the voyage, coming to Gabriel to ask which seemed better to read, words for the burial of a child or those for the burial of the dead at sea. In the end, the words and prayers were mixed and altered to suit the day.

Catherwood helped Mary Silverthorne and the ship's sailmaker to arrange the corpse. They wet the boy's coarse blond hair to make it lie smooth and washed his soiled body. On the thin face, drained of color during his short sickness, a few freckles floated. Mary Silverthorne slipped a worn gimmal-ring threaded with ribbon around his neck. "Some Christian company against the sea elvers and fishes," she said to Catherwood.

"I did mean to be good to John," she added, "not having child of my own."

The sailmaker, Cadabur, arranged the weights, tumbling a length of shattered chain, a broken ringbolt, and a holystone at the boy's bare feet.

"Sea cauls be man sewing," he said, squatting on his heels to stitch the tough canvas envelope, refusing all help with the needle.

On deck, the wind tore Captain Chidgley's words away. Now and again the assembled passengers caught fragments of speech. *O merciful Lord and God our Father, whose shining face the angels of thy little ones do always behold in heaven; Grant us stead-fastly to believe that this thy dear child John Bird, reft from his earthly father and mother, hath winged into the safe nest and keeping of thine eternal love.* Then came the words they waited for, as the captain in a hoarse voice commended the boy's soul to God, committing *his body to the deep.* A pause as the canvas package was tilted from its bed of boards and dropped twisting into the water, an almost soundless splash, and the captain read on, praising that far-off day when the world's foundations would stir and the sea give up its dead. Catherwood held Gabriel's hand beneath her cloak, watching the canvas plunge into sea: a white blur under the green; a shooting stream of bubbles; another; then nothing but whitecapped waves.

Hours later she wondered whether John Bird had yet reached bottom, the sea being so much deeper than a well. Did his body float like a water plant, tethered by his weighted feet, his uplifted arms and hair shifting like tendrils inside his caul? Did the merry, shimmering creatures of ocean dance around him, or was there nothing but shapeless black so far from light and air?

Perhaps he drifted, peacefully clinging to his white sail, following the great sea currents.

The days washed by the same, whether feast or fast, each a round of eating identical meals, washing clothes after the frequent rains. Gabriel and Catherwood read or played cards or visited with their cousins, helping to amuse Sarah de Bruton, who now appeared much further along in pregnancy than previously suspected and who suffered from almost constant seasickness.

On the sixty-second day out, the western sky turned dense with clouds, and for a day the ship sailed without a lull toward a cloud bank that appeared to mount directly out of the sea. Then the air grew still and warm, the ship plowing on through gunmetal waves. At sunset the sun burned weakly in a mud-colored sky, and afterward the stars seemed only frail and fluttering moth lights.

Before dusk fell, Captain Chidgley ordered the few passengers above decks to steerage or to their cabins. Catherwood and Gabriel waited for the storm, rolled in a featherbed, their three men from home sitting cross-legged on the wool bed against the door.

"The chests be lashed tight," Gabriel said.

"There is nothing more to do," Cath whispered. The two newlyweds clutched each other about the waist, listening intently.

A swinging oil lantern cast uneasy halos of light on the walls and ceiling, shining on the men's set faces. Banging noises and shouts could be heard at a distance, then a brief spatter of big raindrops, as though a flock of birds had thudded suddenly against the deck. The wind made the vibrating sound of a string jerked taut, behind it a shriller noise like a band of tin whistles.

"Huh," James Chilcott grunted, thrown against a wall. The ship bucked and plunged, and chests in the tiny cabin shifted and strained at their ropes.

The chamber was flung to one side, then another, the metal lantern reeling. From outside the room came the thumps and battering noises of shifting objects. The unleashed ship skidded into an abyss, crashed into wild walls of waves, and was hurled on as if all the world's winds were suddenly unbottled. The storm drove by on all sides, shrieking and screaming, wrenching the ship in an invisible vise.

Now the trembling lantern circled wildly on its axis.

"Will is hurt," Henry Pasturel cried.

In the maddened, shaking light, Cath caught sight of Will's bleeding cheek, cut by a flying nail. Whistling and crying outside drowned his words.

Cath shook her head.

"Not bad hurt," Will shouted.

"Pull the bed up around your shoulders and heads," Gabriel yelled, wrapping the featherbed close around his wife, drawing it tight around the pair of them.

In an instant they were thrown as one onto the wall, which suddenly, unaccountably, became a wobbling floor, with roped chests threatening to crash down upon them, so that all five, tangled in their sack beds, shouted in alarm. With a lurch the cabin righted itself, and in an unexpected lull they rearranged their beds, wedging themselves in a circle between chests, checking the fastenings and lashings on each chest and box.

"Poor Sarah," Cath said, settling back in

the center of the featherbed. "I hope she is lashed tight."

The lull dissolved in gusts of wind that, shrieking and reeling, whirled the ship like a spindle, knocked it from side to side. All night the passengers stayed awake and wide-eyed, dashed down through abyss after abyss until it seemed they must reach the floor of the sea; flying up toward heaven, buffeted and smashed by hard green thrusts of ocean. Water rushed in every cranny and passage, seeping through cracks, racing to glaze the boards, then flooding back under the door.

Morning came on imperceptibly with a slow brightening, a morning whistling with wind, moaning in abandonment.

For two more days the ship rode choppy seas, wallowing west toward America. On the third day the passengers dared the decks again, collecting rainwater for washing, drying their dank beds, letting the wind blow fear away. Pale and smudged under the eyes, Sarah appeared, leaning on the rail for a few minutes. A bird settled on the mainmast, perching on a cleat to watch the sailors.

"Like we be," Captain Chidgley told Gabriel Lyte. The captain rubbed the aquamarine on his finger for luck. "Blown off course but comfortable after the worst of wind and storm."

Catherwood looked toward the west, league after league of mist and tilting water.

Five more days the ship sailed through rough waters, hulling day after day, drifting under short sail, urged by the wind. On the sixth morning, three land birds unfamiliar to the English flew past, one lighting on the topsail halyards, and in the afternoon Catherwood spied land about ten leagues away. Captain Chidgley informed the passengers that they stood off the cape called Cape James, or Cape Cod; they felt disappointed, like him unwilling to seek harbor so close to dissenters.

"Gentlemen, ladies," he said to the cabin passengers, "we must put in for repairs to the ship. Several beams in the midships bowed during the storm, and the main-topgallant mast is cracked beyond saving. I propose to make harbor at New York on Hudson's river, a port again under English rule, and to remain there for several weeks."

There was nothing to be done; at least the

cabin parties would have the freedom of the town during their stay.

"It is best," Sarah de Bruton told Cath. "This baby pitches and reels most days, though today he is still."

Cath rested a hand on Sarah's shoulder. "Like a ship after storm, cousin," she said.

The ship came about, headed to New York. Catherwood and Gabriel watched the sandy headland and scrub retreat from the ship. A deer fled out of the woods, raced along the shore, then hid itself in the trees.

In late afternoon the ship met with a tangle of shoals, with wind and crashing breakers. Tacking, the ship stood out to sea at nightfall.

"Tomorrow," Captain Chidgley told the Lytes, "we will try again to pass the shoals. They be charted as Point Care, a rough place the Dutch and French call Malabar."

And Malabar was the name Sarah de Bruton wanted to give her son, born the next day just as the ship passed out of the rough breakers and shoals of Malabar. Edmund John de Bruton, named for his father's father, was born just before twilight, during Captain Chidgley's third attempt to breach the shoals. Cath, her cousin Mary de Bruton, Robert and Mary's ward Fan Chancellor, and the sold wife Mary Silverthorne attended the birth, a brutal labor and delivery of seventeen hours, straightforward in its progress save for the rocky seas that twice rolled the laboring woman from her sack bed onto the cabin floor. Catherwood, like the other women in the room, had seen painful childbed deaths. Sick and nauseous for the first time since the ship sailed from Bristol, she cried with relief when the crown with its slick hair showed; twenty minutes later the head shot forward a final time, and then the whole boy, dented and bruised but protesting with vigor, was expelled from Sarah's womb after two hours of hard pushing.

There being no midwife present, Richard de Bruton gave Mary Silverthorne two marks in thanks, and he presented a pair of gloves to each of his three lady cousins.

The women scrubbed the room while Sarah slept with her child in her arms. Catherwood and Mary Silverthorne dumped buckets of childbed clouts into the sea, emptying them well away from the men gathered around Richard de Bruton. Some of the cloth sank and some floated, a red stain spreading on the foaming waters.

"A shame to waste good linen," said Mary Silverthorne, "so near to land."

Afterward Catherwood carried the baby, swaddled, dressed in a gown and crimson mantle, up on deck to give the newborn child fresh from his own salt sea a look at the bigger ocean he had crossed. Richard de Bruton took the child, thanking God for his safe delivery. His brother and the other men congratulated the new father. "A fine, lusty boy," said Robert, holding his nephew. The boy squinted against the streaming salt air, then opened his eyes wide, staring toward the green arc of a wave. A small, neat yawn, and he blinked twice and fell asleep.

"The sea air is good for a child," said Captain Chidgley, clapping Richard de Bruton on the back. "Pray this boy is a good sign for the long and hard bearing pains of a voyage, that we be delivered shortly to York."

"Is York far?" asked Catherwood, reaching for the sleeping child. In a moment she would take him back to Sarah, perhaps with more good news.

Captain Chidgley nodded. "Not far, nor long," he said, "if winds hold prosperous and fair."

New York Letters

June the fifteenth, 1676
To my worthy deare brother Lacey Grevel,
I commend me to you, praying for your good estate and that of your deare son Jamie. We now bide in Neue York city in the Duke of York's propriatarie landes, waiting with great uncertainty the repares to our ship. On our first arrivall we were made to present our names and conditions to the Mayor at City Hall, where we met a Mr. William Selwood, an Oxford friend of Mr. Lytes father, well conneckted with the ruling officers, as well as the English lords and some of the patroons, a sorte of Dutch lord. This gentleman Mr. Selwood helps us greatly. He and my husband go with Robert

and Richard de Bruton and two of our men to inspeck land west of the manor of Rensselaerwyck, and it seems we may settel away from the Virginia countrie, and indede none of us wishes to hazzard our lives so soon on the seas again, after our late dangers of wind and rough storm. This despite that York is a place we did study to avoid, in Bristol hearing wild talk that the Dutch would battle againe for the colonie; also there be ill reports of the overweening greed of York manor lords, such that lesser men may not purchase estates.

We be now grown to a familie of seventeen, having altogether our nine serving men, three married couples, Robert de Bruton's ward, Frances Chancellor, and now Edmund, a quick appearring babe of Sarah de Bruton. We have good hope he will persevere, though small in make. Pray God he do so. Mary tells me Frances is orphan of the great London fire, she afterward passed hand to hand like an unwanted bundle. It makes me fond of her.

This is a prettie lande, and York might be a prettie citie but for a prodigious deal of filth and a bad odour. Littel boys heave stones into the relicks of old Neue Amsterdam canals, which do send out a mortifying stink. Next to the houses, church, the ordinaries, pier, and everie where the stretes be thick with waggons and *carts and sledges, with stacks of gravel or cobbles and timbers. Altogether the scene dont attract, full of livelie dangers from men drunk with West Indies rum or sober who whip their beastes and snorte about the town at high speede. The fort stands higgledie-piggledie, overrambled by citizens not of the better sorte—in short by hogges and barrow-pigs who tusk about the earthenworks and over-topple the palisadoes. And indede a visitor spies out these Grillish citizens run amuck throughout the city. The neue governour Andros, a militarie man and a supporter of the king, has a fine battle ahead with swine and dirt.*

The city is a regular Babell of tongues, with upward of eighteen languages spoke, and a deal of animal noise beside. After endurring an unclene English inn, we removed to a Dutch house, a nice, tidie place overseen by a woman who knows the York herbs and who speakes a good kind of English, despite that she can not so much as signe her name in anie language. Everie day is feast day here, with spicy deer meat or turkey, dry and of a fine flavour, or a rackoon, a fatty animal tasting of pork. Each Dutch lady is addickted to pickled oysters, dugge up all along the lower Henry Hudson river and Long Island shore, some of them being two handes in lenth, and it is a small in-

dustrie here to digg oysters and pickle the meate, then burne the shells to lime. The pantries here be row on row full of dried apples and grapes and other plentie.

The Dutch ladies seem a compleat change from our own, being unloosed to buy and sell, bargan and make contracks and leeve their jointures where they will. And praised as shrewd in busyness of all kindes. Mr. Lytes cozzens behave like English loyals in disdaning them and manye others besides, as manye Dutch do disdane us in kind, but indeed theym women of some interest. While I see a deal of rickettie thatched huts, others of these Dutch live in fine brick houses, gabled, of glazed and unglazed bricks mixed, with prettie pictured or colored tilework sprinkled out-of-doors and in, and with a small, clean raised flore outside the doores that they call stoope. A neat people, the women wear snowie head dresses and seem fond of colored stones set in goldwerk. Like all the colonials in York, their teeth go most terribly shattered by eating of honey and much West Indies sugar in sweetmeats, and even by a tree sap that the Indians boil into sweet sirrups. We do often observe the wives spredding linens on the bleeching ground, a wide grasse plat near this house. Some English tell us that the Dutch women wait out the winter perched on warming *pans which they keep freshened with live coles, hawling up their petticotes to shovell in the fire, and smoaking their long Dutch pipes all the whiles. Also they tell tales that this heat makes the Dutch ladies to brede a livelie small creature called a* sooterkin.

We hear that Fort Orange is a reckless spot, and the Dutch farmers and others who live such near bedfellows to the Indians go more wildly, being unfettered and too proud to be governed by church or officiall. It seems that too easie a path to cider and West Indies rum leads them all astray, even the Dutch churchmen. I do pray our men return safe from these forrest places. They now go west of Rensselaerwyck.

And now I must go as well, to do my dutie by cozzen Sarah, who continues in an uneasie way. My afectionate greetings to our old familie, not forgetting our Gaffer Withycombe, who should know that many prettie Dutch gardens grow in York but none so pleasant as his own. Our Henry Pasturel desires to be remembered by all, especially to his mother and to Gaffer Tap and to Margarett Withycombe. I shall send directions for posting with my next letter, and do not fale to write me, deare brother, for I long for a glance at home, a peep in the hall and garden walks. It is not least in my mind to say,

I hope you may wish me and Mr. Lyte joy next Februarie. I do miss our mother more than ever now.

> *Adieu, my mothers childe.*
> *Youre afectionate sister,*
> *Catherwood Anne Lyte*

To think that an ocean stood between Catherwood and her mother's grave! This man Gabriel, whom she liked more and more, must be family and home to her—Lacey and Jamie beyond the sea, her mother dead. Here, in the mud of new streets, the rooms and walks of Grevel House were fragments of a lost world.

Cath rolled the quill in her ink-stained fingers, dreaming of home, remembering how she had eavesdropped on her mother.

"He may not go to Virginia, once he has a wife so near to his own family," Mrs. Grevel had said.

"It id'n certain, surely," said Lacey Grevel.

Now, Cath thought, she could marry if she wished, changing her life with Elisabeth's gift of a marriage portion. Could make her own decision, yes or no, although she knew that marriage remained the best, the safest future for a young woman with few connections. To leave her mother, that would be the difficult thing. If only she could keep Elisabeth always with her! It was unlikely that Mrs. Grevel would live to great age, given her frequent weakness and ill health, and her death would leave Cath alone save for Lacey and his small son. Lacey, the man she loved best in the world, would be hunting around his estates for another wife, a small heiress to some of the last century's wool fortunes or cousin to a lord, one who would add to the family luster. So much the better if she acted as a second mother to his son. Really there was not much choice; if not this man, her mother's choice, then some other, perhaps less pleasing.

"But what sort of name is that?" Lacey asked. "Gabriel Trevarthan Lyte. Trevarthan—so awkward and foreign. Cornish."

"Hush," said Elisabeth, "hush. Lyte is a good, mannerly family."

Only a month later, Cath glanced at the young man leaning with one arm propped on the mantel, talking about Virginia to Elisabeth's rector, George Arundel. "This island of England a bridge," quoted Mr. Arundel, "a gallery to the New World." Mr. Lyte nodded, his face alert and attentive. The third son of a clergyman at Wells and cousin to their de Bruton neighbors, he was the one for whom little could be provided, who meant to brave the passage to America.

Elisabeth had presented Gabriel Lyte to Catherwood only a few moments before. Cath had had time to ascertain only that his eyes were blue as he held her gaze with a careful, examining look—not the brief, merry greeting of Lacey's fashionable friends.

The New World, she thought; he would be sailing to the land of wild men where there were no pleasant deer parks and chases but only gigantic trees bigger than any trees in England, dripping with vines and noisy with strange birds and monkeys.

Cath carried her cup to a window, reflecting on Elisabeth's pleasant drawing room, with its pale green walls and broad ovolo molding, and thinking that in the New World surely there would be no rooms like this one with its multi-light windows looking down onto a trim park, bounded by a neat row of pales.

A shadow fell across the glass.

"Mr. Arundel says that he should like me to bring him seeds of Indian tabac from the

New World. And you? What would you like?"

Startled, Cath looked into the young man's face. He was handsome as a man who is strong and straight and full of health is handsome, and his eyes were bright, intent on hers.

"Medicinal seeds for his herbary, I suppose." She paused and turned slightly away from him. "Indeed, I do not know, Mr. Lyte. It is picturesque, the Virginia country, is it not?" Cath looked across to the shrubbery walk. "Wild, I think, compared with our forests and woodlands?"

"Certainly wild. But beautiful, if all reports be true."

"Then I should like a handful of foreign feathers," she said thoughtfully.

"No more than that?"

"I could not say. Surely nothing new of value has yet come back to us here but tobacco. And I do not love a pipe. Perhaps a green-and-yellow-striped monkey who would cling on my wrist," she said, looking at him slantwise.

Of course he laughed. Of course there were no monkeys. She had known there would be no green and yellow monkeys, but she had been quite sure of brown ones with the whiskered faces of old men, which latched onto the Virginia trees with their tails, blinking at the hot new sun with amber eyes.

"Perhaps our planters simply ain't found your monkeys yet," said Gabriel Lyte. "Surely we could be surprised at nothing that came out of America."

The thirtieth day of July, 1676
To my deare brother Lacey Grevel,

I commend me unto you, hoping that you and my deare nevue Jamie be in good state and have safe receit of my letter. Thus far we do congratulate ourselves on this luckie change from Virginia to York, that after resking our bodies at sea and river we come to a good port of rest, a beautiful fair place with tall trees and many stremes, so that my husband and cozzens projeck a saw mill to rive planks on the east end of this land when they can obtain a skillfull mason and a Daneland or German joiner, who knowes the making of water wheeles. By the abel intercession of Mr. Selwood we own each outright a large parsel of wooded landes. We continue well, onlie Sarah going so weak as to be no help in settling our houses, which, sett severally apart in aban-

doned fields of the Indians, make littel show of substance. Indede, we slepe more like badgers in holes than like gentelmen and ladies, our first houses being dugg cellars higher than a man, the walls well cased with smallish timbers and bark, the flore of packed erth, the roof being trunks of thin whole trees covered with sod. Not long hereafter we will have a true house of rooms and planch floor, having compackted with Mr. Lytes cozzens to hire John Torkillus, a Swede joiner, to frame three houses in October. We will be right glad to leave both earth and tree and coarse wether behind doors. This house of ours can then be cellar. Chests and cases be all our furniture, our tabel, bench, and chair. Upon rising, I toss linens and feather bedd on a chest and am done with house cleaning.

So you may see that we must putt away dances and gold lace until a later day, bending our care to warm burrows, mattocks, and spades, for in truth we go very busie with werk of all kindes, doing above a bit more labor than I should care to admitt to any gentleman but my own brother. Will Pasturel means to undertake a plow of ashwood some day latterly, after he and Henry manage a linhay and a barn for cattle and to store our tooles and thresh grain. The trees all around be girdled alreddie, that is, stripped of nurishing bark so that they wither and die dailie, a sadd sight to see but gladd for planting our grain from England and also York corn seed, which in the next year we mean to plant about with pumpkin and beans as the Indians do. For this year Mr. Lyte further projecks a house of hall and parlor and low bedchambers, a smokehouse, and some cleered ground.

Our land seems a healthfull spot, not humoursome or unwholesome: in Neue York, our Dutch landlady held it as doctrine that Virginia is a woebegone colonie of swamps and insects, and a very feverish, sickly countrie of tertian agues, few among the Virginia people living to see their children full grown. So Mr. Lyte and me be glad and thankfull to God not to have come there, it being a strange surprizing fortune that did bear us here. Although I feer her too much partiall, as she boasted of the place as a deal more helthie than anie countrie in Europe.

We be nigh to the Iroquoi or the Five Nations, Indian tribes who seem well respected for industrie and fierceness by both Dutch and English. They bidd fair to conquer all the Indians hereabouts, having late subdued the Suskque Hannocks to the south. It seemes theym great traders and hunters, and their women farmers, although farming much fallen away during these last years of war and trade. One rover stopped by our house—our Den, I shall call it— a handsome tall traveller dressed in a lether hunt shirt, leggings, and high sided slippers that tyed in front, with fine marks running catercorner across his face and a knott of hair on his head called a "scalp lock," meant to teaze his enemie with a taunting handel to grasp. However it was, I courted peace by serving round dishes of London tea. In Albanie rumors fly of a battel in Neue England between the tribes there and the English settlers, mostly dissenters. Some say the Indians be utterlie massacred. Others say that their great sachem that we call King Phillip raids the English from his hiding places in swamps and forrests. We heard report that the Neue England Indians will disembowl a great-bellied woman and thrust the babe in her womb on a split like a pig, but whether they leave the child for a sign or truely roste and eat it, I know not. And many suchlike stories whether truth or dildram be told of them. I was minded of the pitifull man we saw drawn and quartered in peeces at Bristol, despite there being no comparrison as to cause.

I pray, do not concern your self as to my comfort, for this is a handsome land and I in compleat content with my lott. My ladie cozzens do appeare in uneasie wise as to our present living, looking tremblingly to the future, expeckting some unbeknownst, momentarie dizaster, but I thank God that we was led to be independent of help in this countrie, finding my current hardshippes not too troubelsome. I beleve my husband fitt for this place in vigour and strong purpose, and a better friend, more afectionate and observant of my wishes, I could not desire.

In three days time he will dispatch this letter, goeing to Albanie for oxbeasts, two clean-timbered horses, a painted bedsted alreddy bespoke, tool irons, and sundrie other needs to be gathered by our agent, and I hope we shall not be cheated like the natives as we have good English angels. I be gladd to stop at home, and will not willingly go so far as York again for some time, for I never saw such sadd tacking about of boates as on Henry Hudsons river, such tidall swelles give place to dead calmes with pestering flies mazing about in air, so that I should be gladd to stay away from all water and from York citie and Albanie as well. If Neue York is a town of filth and clean tile, everie man and woman a shopkeep of pins and needles or taback and rum, then Albanie is a town of muck and fur and more rum, with thatch and board huts thrown around the forte like so many mushrooms reared up overnight in a grazing ground.

Our men from home continue a great help and comfort to us, and desire to be comended to all our old familie householde. Mr. Lyte presented them with young pigges and lande to till on their own account.

I bid you an afectionate adieu, with prayers for your good helth and content, continueing to miss most sorely my deare Mrs. Elisabeth Grevel, for counsel and sweetness, a mother without her equall. Mr. Lyte bids me send greetings, his best service, and assurances that my helth holds strong.

Your respectful and loving sister,
Catherwood Grevel Lyte

Labor and the Garden

Catherwood's vegetable and herb garden, unpacked from rags and a chest of seeds and roots, was a parcel of her adopted mother's manor, a plot of Somerset. Every seed or root had its genesis in her mother's garden, each plant shepherded by Gaffer Withycombe. The old man ruled the ground and his store of sets and seeds. He spooned out seeds for Catherwood, some fine as gunpowder grains, some big as shed milk teeth, others large coarse buttons. Each scoop of seed was labeled in Cath's hand, each packaged in slips of paper torn from a discarded pamphlet. She would not plant most of the seeds until the next spring; others would not bloom and fruit for several years. In her New World burrow, Cath pressed a few of the folded sheets back open, stacking them neatly for later use.

One by one, even grain by grain, Cath buried the seeds and roots in raised earth, painstakingly soaking the beds with water. Not every seed sprouted, and some made up only a stunted miniature landscape of leaves. In August three court pendu plat apple trees were only sticks. A damask rose put out a few stingy leaves.

"My mother did love that rose."

"Another year or two," Gabriel said, "if we guard it from animals."

Cath thought of Gaffer Withycombe's stand of damasks, dewy in morning, streaming with perfume when the sun warmed the garden. *Rose blowth.* A gardener at Grevel House since boyhood, Gaffer Withycombe claimed that there was no rose more fragrant than the *Pompom des Princes.* In spring the thin-stemmed plant was a green light-absorbing fountain of leaves, but at midsummer it became a shining rosy cataract, the weakly tethered blossoms flinging themselves wildly out and down, heedless of fall. Fuddled, in love with the silk-lipped petals, bees tumbled from leaves and flowers, catching themselves in midair and zinging erratically away or plummeting to the grass blades. By summer's end hundreds of slim bristly hips dangled from the bent and broken canes.

But Cath's New World garden was ripe, piled high with rich soil. By the end of August the first flowers bloomed, and leaves frilled or hairy or broad burgeoned on the black ground. Where wild clematis mounted a nearby maple, Cath wove a bower of willow withies, shaping an arch over a rough seat for two, coaxing the vine down to the curved roof.

Just behind the garden were logs, adzed into rectangles, meant for timber frames. A pit and heaps of pit-sawn lumber lay farther back. Gabriel and the other men took turns with the bottom end of the long two-man saw, as they all hated the hot work in the pit, sawdust and chips and another man's sweat showering down. Earlier they had leveled the ground, clearing away scrub and trees. Then Gabriel had laid out the three bays of the house, hammering pegs into the earth with a mallet.

When the house was framed and built, the garden walk would lead to the front stairs, and from the rooms they could look out on herbs and vegetables, then beyond to a fine view of rolling land, fields, and a stream curling along a valley.

"This land is strange as the sea," Gabriel said.

"The country is flowing and beautiful," Cath agreed.

The undulating landscape was weather-tossed, the sun every day rearing white in an illuminated cloud over the wild hills, as though thrusting itself forward over the ridges, a sight new and almost fearful. Each morning Cath told over her prayers while seated on a stump, staring at that burning veil. Rain and lightning blew across the valley, and day and night unfamiliar cries broke the forest's seeming calm.

After Gabriel told Cath about the traveling dissenter he and Henry Pasturel had met in Albany, she became even more observant of the landscape. A hunched Puritan dressed in leather doublet and hose, he followed the two men down a muddy lane, whispering in a hoarse voice of the unicorns he saw frolicking in woods beyond the Hudson. Cath watched for their pale sides flashing between the trees, watched for the wild brown warriors slipping through the underbrush. Birds made fearful shrieks, great flocks flying so thick that Cath heard whistles and the multiplied rush of wings. Then an almost random shot, another: ducks or pigeons plunged from the heights. Torn from the limp birds, the green, blue, gold, and russet-brown feathers drifted back into the air or twirled and caught along the tops of low grasses and leaves.

The whole world was fresh and curious to Catherwood, and there were times that she felt herself the newest of all created things, shiny as a just-minted coin. When she gazed into a white pillar of morning clouds or watched with Gabriel as the huge cloud-burdened sky burned with sunset, when she saw a quick half-hidden movement among the trees, when she felt the first fishtail flutter of the child, then she vibrated with anticipation like a plucked string.

Long before her womb rounded out, Catherwood's longing for the child was born and grew, until it more than matched the homesickness she felt for her brother and Grevel

House. The stems periscoping out of earth, untwisting their leaves, stretching them farther and farther out until every cell rejoiced in sun: every tendril and flower spoke to her of things to come. She was quite certain of a daughter, although she never spoke of her certainty, feeling words to be needless or perhaps unlucky.

"Do you want only boys, like Richard and Robert?" she had asked Gabriel. They were lying in the featherbed, and she turned away from him, unsure of what he might say.

He pressed against her back, one hand on her belly, his breath on her neck.

"You and a healthy child, sound in mind and limb."

By late August she was ripening, her stomach swelling with the proof of things unseen. Sleepy with summer and growth, she dozed every afternoon in the bower, dropping the hoe where she stood and stumbling to the bench, or else curling up on a bed rug. Autumn seemed to wake Cath, astonishing her with its strength of color. She and Gabriel waded in the leaf fall, picking up big motley maple leaves and sticking them in each other's hair, laughing and rolling together in the bright, dry drifts.

"My wife is a sprite. A lovely leaf-crowned nymph of the woods."

"And soon a lovely round Indian pumpkin," Catherwood said, lying on her back in leaves. Reaching up, grasping Gabriel's black hair in both hands, she saw herself reflected small, coined in his eyes.

"We be 'looking babies,' " he said, seeing his face mirrored in Cath's eyes.

Cath gave a one-sided smile, feeling light-headed with desire. Gabriel already seemed to know what she was thinking. She had heard of such things, when an arranged marriage proved good, as sometimes happened. No longer did she find herself dreaming about her adopted brother, about staying forever at Grevel House. Instead she remembered lying naked in the long grass, Gabriel feeding her with small grainy strawberries. Or the burrow at night with his hair against her cheek, his heart pounding like a mallet against her own.

"More than looking, Gabriel."

The harvest was almost in, purchased grain and Indian corn stored in two great sacks, the remainder heaped in rude baskets along the walls of their dirt house or packed in a cellar dug nearby. Cath had been the one to dig and sow and pick, to dry wild berries, and even to weave the baskets: now she took pleasure in the sight of her makeshift pantry, complete save for kale, cabbages, and some of the root crops still in the ground.

There were even fresh seeds and pumpkins, gained by bartering with Indians camped to the south. One morning five young men emerged from the forest, squatting on their heels to drink sweetened tea while Gabriel Lyte presented them with a box of colored ribbons. From one of these men they learned that the war in New England was over. "Battle over," he said, pointing east. "Metacomet," he said, slicing at his throat with a finger. A few days later four of the men reappeared with the pumpkins and a basket of seeds, staying again to eat hearth cakes. The new seeds filled Cath's folded papers: a variety of Indian bean, some particolored Indian corn, and pumpkin seeds. Wedges of pumpkin meat lay sweetening on boards in the sun.

Finally the work in the saw pit was ended, James and Will celebrating by throwing Henry into the hole half-filled with leaves. In the cool evenings the family sat around a bonfire, hammering nails. Soon John Torkillus would come to direct the framing of a house and barn, and then there would be a flurry of work to finish the walls and roof.

Like a coin with one side a delicate and lively head, the other a death mask, the harvest and coming birth showed two faces to Catherwood. As the days rolled on toward winter and childbirth, she wavered between anticipation and fear.

Cath could remember the very hour when she knew she was pregnant, detecting a sweet cloying smell on her skin and in her urine. For an instant she had felt a surge of joy, before her old fear of a harsh death took hold and mingled with her happiness. She had seen one of her mother's tenants die in childbed, after a local midwife had used a thatcher's hook to pull the dead baby from her womb. Alice de Cheltenham, one of Mrs. Grevel's nearest neighbors, had died in paroxysms, her back and neck scoured red with rashes, only a week after bearing a son. Her eyes, shiny with pain, had traveled around the room, unable to rest.

Often Cath had seen a swaddled baby, a seven- or eight-month child washed clean of blood and vernix, eyelids closed, lying in a basket. She remembered her mother, stroking a young girl's forehead, promising to supply her with cakes and beer for a baby's funeral, trying to comfort her. "In a year or more, surely the Lord will raise up more children for your joy. For now we must find solace that all things do show us God's will."

Even if a child lived, there was no surety. So many of her mother's family stories were about death—the three daughters and their grandmother dead with the red cross of plague ruddled on the door, a husband dead at Edgehill, a father and two younger sisters destroyed by smallpox. She herself was a child raised up for her mother's comfort, a gift when there seemed no chance of further children.

There were so many memories of childbirth death. Her brother Lacey's wife, Frances Weoley, who had brought Lacey eight thousand pounds and a country manor in Gloucestershire. Her first lying-in came at Grevel House, ten months after the marriage, when she was still fifteen. Mrs. Grevel and Cath attended her, along with maids and Mrs. Anne Rice, daughter of a doctor and educated by her father in Latin so that she could study anatomy and medicine. After a morning of vomiting and weeping, Fanny appeared spent. Her labor ran on through the night and following day before Mrs. Rice managed to turn the baby. Mrs. Grevel's maid Ursula asked Fanny to pray, and when the girl could not speak, prayed loudly that she *be delivered from the pain the Lord laid upon her for disobedience, being descended from the loins of Eve*. The cries from Mrs. Grevel's bed grew faint but hoarse, the breath rasping in and out until the prolonged high pitched cries as the child was turned. Then came increasing contractions and several hours of ceaseless pushing before the crown with its swirled dark hair could be seen. The baby, hauled safely from her body, was a boy, battered and purple-faced but alive and yelling while his face was wiped clean. Fanny wept helplessly when Mrs. Rice gave thanks for a live and perfect baby, then fell asleep before she delivered the after-burden.

Lacey hired a wet nurse for the baby Jamie, although his mother urged against it. He did not want his wife to be burdened by the unclean, troublesome practice, and even Mrs. Rice spoke against suckling as bad for the health. But a man should not go to his wife while she nursed a babe, Mrs. Grevel explained to Cath. Three months later Frances found herself pregnant, and she confided to Cath that she had no hope of living through such a trial again. No talk of cradles and baskets, swaddling clothes, and baby mantles could entice her. "Grandmother Eve would not make thee suffer so again," Lacey told his wife, teasing, but Cath feared for her new sister, praying for her constantly.

Her pregnancy ended abruptly with hemorrhage and the delivery of a stillborn doll of a baby, coated with vernix but complete even to transparent eyelashes and brows. It was a girl. "Maybe one of our kind will be more valued in the kingdom of heaven," Mrs. Grevel said, the baby in her arms.

Mrs. Rice attended Fanny, but not even lancing and cupping stopped the flow.

"The pain is not so bad now, and I be ready to stay or go. Indeed, all resigned to God's will," Fanny whispered to Cath.

"My dear sister," Cath said, "stay."

Fanny dwindled in the big bed, growing whiter and whiter as Ursula carried basin after basin of childbed clouts from the room.

At the end her breath was slight, shallow: gone.

October thirtieth, 1676
To my deare brother and friend Lacey Grevel,
I commend me to your afection and prayers, hoping that you and my sweet nephue Jamie be in good helth and spirits. As yet I can not expeckt to hear from home but have great hopes of a letter some day soon, and this I sende by my cozzen Robert de Bruton, who travels with one of his men to Albanie this week. The weather hereabout begins to show sharp and lustie, so we be all thankfull to God that our Swede man has come and mortized a tight timber frame house for us. James Chilcott rough-cut wide shingel boardes for us. Mr. Lyte and the men did saw boardes and hew tree for our house all the summer long, broadaxing the trees while freshe and greene, so that each lay strait and squared on four sides, ready for our Swede man, who we payed in gold coin to come north and cut the mortisses and tennons, to help us to a neat warm house. After some bickerment and the benefitt of more coin, he bided by the plans we did mean for a Virginia house and made our York house just as we desired.

In many a way other than the materiall, this house resembels our manor near Glastonbury, although saddly lacking in stone save for a good mortarred base of field and river stone, for which we much creditt our men, handie and ablish beyond our hope, the Pasturels having receeved much tallent in building of all kindes from Gaffer Pasturel. So our wilde house is a littel Grevel House, with a great sommer hall running from front to back door, and a stairs of brick of our own devise layde in a prettie Garden bonde, leadding up to the front. A room lies on either hande, hall and parlor. We have two large low rooms good for sleeping, one with a closett for our neue bedd, a bigg bedd with posts of four hand spans about at the base and seven feet wide with a trundel cot below, such that we be readie for what companie may come to us, whether friendes or children. At either gabel end we fashioned a great chimnie of sturdie English bonde, cheerfull warm heartes to heate us through the winter, which we feare will prove cruell.

One day we hope to clad the house in brick or stone, and Henry Pasturel projects to plane moldings for doors and windows, some fitted with glasse from home, and some shuttered over until we obtain more glass or lights of horn to fill them. So farre our rooms stand near emp-

tie, having only our chests, bedd, and a board tabel.

As you maye well guess, Mr. Lyte and I must help our men in these neue endeavors, firing brick or axing logs, though we find some leizure to be gentle man and ladie. Please tell Gammer Withycombe that we forrest dwellers have gone together to contrack with an English churchman to visit us three times a year, for the holy communion and for whatever sacraments and offices be needfull, and that we cozzens have altogether built a small chapell, a sort of closett for worship, where he may marry or baptize. Also, we do keep very steadily the morning and evening prayers with our men, so that God should not be neglected even in the wilds.

My deare brother, pray God we meet again in this life, for I do miss the merrie wayes of Lacey Grevel, not having forgot the sweetness and joyfullness you showed unto me all my life. It is cruel to think that you will never hold and admire a new minted child of mine. Jamie must now grow strong and boisterous. I long to play with him in the little wilderness beside Grevel House, where we never yet feared of Indians, nor hoped to see a unicorn.

Youre afectionate and homelonging sister,
Catherwood Grevel Lyte

Late fall was no time of ease. Although the men now saw to the milking as well as their usual barn chores, tending to the oxen and horses, chasing pigs out of the woods where they had rooted for mast all summer long, for Catherwood there remained the mending and making of work clothes, the cooking of meals and cleaning. After the loft was finished, Henry took over the washing of clothes, boiling them out of doors in a big pot they had brought from New York, and James turned out butter and rammel cheeses as handily as any dairymaid. Gabriel undertook to make five pairs of high-sided slippers to wear in snow, similar to some moccasins he had seen Indians wearing.

Indians were a worry, although after peaceful encounters with stray Iroquois, and after repeated evidence that the war in New England was over, they felt more at ease. Gabriel was determined that they learn to be good shots, in the event of attack, so the men stayed busy with hunting. They made a few pit and deadfall traps and cured pelts for sale.

But no season was all work, the three families now meeting more frequently, traveling away from home to spend a day, often staying overnight. Since Cath could no longer ride, she walked with Gabriel or one of the other men. Occasionally she went through the fields and woods alone, following a broken line of ax marks on the trees. The three women and Fan, Robert de Bruton's ward, used their leisure time to stitch baby linen and warm infant clothes. Mary's first baby appeared to be due in Advent, and Cath expected her first in February.

"A baby needs a monstrous amount of linen," said Mary. It must be true, thought Cath, for it seemed to her that Sarah's washpot always boiled behind the house.

On chilly days the women cut and sewed around the fireplace, but on sunny days they carried a bed rug outside and sewed on the grass. Baby Edmund would lie on his back, clouds reflected in his round eyes. When Cath held the child, she imagined the two babies sitting close together, one unborn, separated from the other only by a narrow wall. Perhaps someday they would marry, there being few choices of their own kind in New York. The baby loved the bright leaves, arching his back to get a better look at the crisp shapes against the sky. "Da," he said, his eyes roving from oak to maple, "da." He was harvest-plump, with red chapped cheeks and a shock of untamable hair.

Catherwood sang to the baby, watching his pupils widen with interest:

Robin and Richard, twin pretty men,
Bide in bed till clock strikes ten.
Up starts Robin and peeps at sky.
"O brother Dick, the sun climbs high."

Sarah and Mary laughed.

"Quite the gentlemen, to sleep so late," Sarah said.

"Or beggars," Mary added.

The last leaves rocked to the ground, and Catherwood stitched on, working baby clothes—white smocks and gowns, crimson and yellow outer garments. Most were useful plain garments save for their fine materials. Later on she might find time for lace and embroidery, but for now she made only a fine green velvet mantle cut from a gown that had belonged to her mother, lining it with embroidered yellow silk.

Finikin work, she thought, that her mother would have admired.

A Feast-Day Story
and the Trapper's Tree

November twenty-second, her first supper for guests in the completed house: Catherwood managed a white fricassee—a hare cooked Dorset fashion, simmered in a skillet with a handful of sweet herbs—next to it a mess of winter greens with salted pork, and a cake cooked on the hearth. The cousins played at cards in the parlor, drinking so much that Henry Pasturel, sitting in the corner by the hall fire, undertook to mix more beer and rum and molasses, branding the flip with a red-hot iron so that it foamed and Fan ran to watch.

"Tell a story," Fan begged, hauling baby Edmund onto her lap. "They won't mind us, for Robert is only watching the others play and don't need another hand."

"Da," Edmund said.

Cath sat down on a stool, thinking that sometimes she felt more comfortable with Henry and Fan than with Mary and Sarah and their husbands. She was no better than Henry by birth; she had been wanted no more than Fan. She admitted herself to be a lucky young woman, but she was also another girl, one who had been bought as casually as a peddler's trinket, a toy or a ribbon.

"Yes, I will tell one," she said, "a fairy story."

And so Henry and Fan listened to Catherwood's tale and remembered it long after.

"Once long ago," Cath began, settling nearer the fire, as though she could find, as storytellers often have, adventure in the flames.

"Once very long ago," she amended, "there did live a beautiful lady, so surpassing lovely and valorous a lady that none could meet or match her in courage and goodness, and as this was a mortal long time ago, before old Eden was all forgot, she could, with the fluent motion of a soul known to God, fly above the meadows and trees and light where she would. And this she did, whenever the impulse filled her up and cast her into the heavens. One day she had the misfortune to light down in a bold bare field where a man, handsome like a devil, with a fierce dominant eye and no heart but a black heart for maidens, snatched her up and kissed this beautiful lady on the lips, bearing her into his silk tent, where he stripped her naked as a pin and ravished this good lady of her honor."

"What was his name?" Fan asked, curling close to Cath.

"Grevel, I think," she said slowly.

"But that is your own name—for such a wicked man."

"No matter that—plenty of Grevels of many kinds in the world, all of us mortals being sinners. The name is of a fine devilish make, now that I think on it."

"Then what was her name?"

"She was such a good lady, so close to the days when angels swooped over our gardens and nested like birds in our trees and castle tops, that she needed no name at all, but some who were less good than she titled her Alma."

Henry spat in the fire, shifting in his seat and bending closer to the women.

"The lady turned bright-eyed and wasting, caught in that tent, turned slender and transparent as a burning beeswax taper. Outside Grevel fought and vanquished each knight who would come to her rescue. A great curled tree hung over his rude throne, and the canopy of thick knotted branches smoked and scorched day and night with his wickedness.

" 'If you will not rue your evil, I must leave you,' the lady told him, but Grevel could neither let her go nor think to leave her.

"One morning she gave him a gift drawn from her sleeve, a burnished Damascus glass warm to the touch. 'When I be gone, you may go to the glass, and so long as I live, you will find it warm to your hand,' she said. She gave him the glass because, despite a year of sorrow, there was yet a man in him to love, buried beneath the ill knight's guise; then just after she spoke, four spirits lifted and bore her away in a white cloth of samite, so that he could do nothing, seeing her no more again, not there, neither in any other place."

Cath paused.

"Ah," Henry said.

"And then what fortune came to them next?" Fan asked.

"I do not know; indeed, that is more than I dreamed," Cath said, smiling.

"You must finish, you must." Fan leaned forward, letting Edmund roll from her lap.

"Abah," Edmund said.

"Henry, will you please serve round the flip?" Cath poked up the fire, then took the baby onto her knees.

"I was just going." He got up, leaving Cath and Fan crouched before the fire.

"Da bah," Edmund said, butting his head against Cath's bodice.

Cath brushed some shreds of bark from her gown. "I must go, Fan. Come and play at cards with us? I must see to their content."

The first deep snow put an end to the women's visits. Ribbed, bubbly icicles climbed head downward from the eaves of house and outbuildings, suddenly diving and shattering into pieces. Clinker-vells, they called them back home but never saw them so many or so large.

"Gooseberry glass," Henry said.

Winter was bitter. During Advent the streams froze, so that even fetching water became difficult, and the air remained brutally cold for weeks at a time.

"Like nail rods be shoved up our noses," James complained.

Each snowfall had its own character, sometimes wet and deep, clumping on branches, unexpectedly plunging from trees and house. More often it was dry, sifting sideways from the sky, sometimes wheeling down in galaxies of joined stars.

To Cath, the winter was like one long evening, the short days sinking into a deep blue twilight. In these dark afternoons, the hall grew companionable, almost festive. Herbs gave a sweet aroma to the room. Often there was a pot of porridge, steaming and sulking on the fire, occasionally thumping with bubbles and spattering the bricks. Or a fricassee of venison might simmer with claret and eggs after Gabriel returned from a morning's hunt. Successful with his leather boots, he turned to deerskin jackets, punching his needle through tanned hide. He recited poems he had memorized from miscellanies and songbooks; after a while the men would ask for "She sat and sewed that hath done me the wrong" and "Madame, withouten any words" and "Willow, willow, sing all of green willow." They liked stories about Eden and Noah and Jonah and anything with fighting against man or God. Gabriel read from the Bible or told the stories from memory, giving the prophets and heroes conversations that made the men laugh. Before going to bed, Gabriel wrote in his diary, telling Cath that "the child will know how we planted a home in the New World, with God's help."

During the slow winter afternoons Henry and Will came inside to plane moldings, the brothers facing the fire and sweeping dust and scraps directly into the flames. Now and then Henry copied out the alphabet on a piece of kindling, using lampblack for ink. Cath was teaching him to write, but Will would not bother, saying that a crisscross was enough for him. He whittled spoons or toys when he sat by the fire. James, morose in the long dark, departed for bed as soon as evening prayers ended. Every night after the Pasturel brothers left the hall, Gabriel and Cath sat close together by the fire, Gabriel with one hand resting on his wife's belly, feeling their child ripple and play against his fingers. "Like she is a swimmer," he said, "in the waving sea." Together they read Mrs. Sharp's *The Midwives Book*. "Though it is woman's business, the day may catch us early and unready, with bearing pains and no woman by to help," Gabriel said.

On Twelfth Night, Robert brought Fan as a gift for Cath's lying-in, boldly riding his horse up the snowy steps and swinging the girl down to the sill. "You will be glad to have her well enough when the day comes," he said to Gabriel, "though she's seen but two births. Still, she is a woman, and we men inherit no great skill in such matters."

He swept in the hall, sniffing the pot on the fire, draining a goblet dry in one gulp. "I be the father of a thumping boy, three days before Christmas," he declared, demanding congratulations.

"Mary—how goes it with Mary?" Cath asked. She slid her arm around Fan's waist. Fan was the little girl-wife in reserve, and if

Mary died, Fan would be made a stepmother and wife.

"Well enough," Robert said, "and the boy John looks a strapper."

"His hair is red as fire, stands up on his poor head like flames," Fan told Cath, burying her head on the older woman's shoulder. Catherwood could feel her shaking with laughter.

Cath and Gabriel exchanged glances, trying not to smile.

"Red hair is worse in a woman, Fan," Robert said. "That a boy go wild and hot is no great matter."

He stayed to dine, then rode off in early afternoon with a promise that his brother Richard would bring Sarah when Cath's labor began, if one of their men could come with the news. Fan and Cath watched him disappear from view, the lively bay mare kicking up streamers of snow. "I be glad of Mary's health," Cath murmured. She hugged Fan. "And glad for your company, little cousin."

Unwearied, the clouds let down storm after storm of snow in January and early February. One night Cath got up, leaving Gabriel's warm curve and the shelter of bed curtains and valance, the big counterpane of yellow camlet that had belonged to her mother. She stepped around Fan, asleep in the trundle bed. Her belly felt tight, her skin a hot sheath.

She waded out in a dry, hissing snow to the trapper's tree where the men hung animals for safekeeping before they were skinned. A fisher, a kind of great weasel, black as ebony, with pearly teeth and a few white wisps among the long and faintly crinkled fur, twirled slowly from a hempen rope beside a bobcat, its stippled markings crisp in the starlight, the bludgeon mark on its nose a single purple berry. "Dear Christ, this world shows very lovely-fierce," Cath whispered.

Discrete stars of snow slanted past, now and again catching and holding to the fisher's midnight fur. Cath closed her eyes. Indians and unicorns fled through the night forests, each as fabulous as the other. Far to the south slumbered Virginia's malarial kingdom of small farmers and artisans, indentured servants, and slaves. They slept dreamless and weary while planters and their children stepped in intricate dances, sacred and profane, under the graceful spinning wheel of the zodiac, under the rooftree of heaven. East, where the sleepless dissenters transcribed the world of wonders into their pained, vacillating diaries, mermaids and spirited sea beasts jostled together under Massachusetts Bay. Outside in the threatening Indian dark lay the black and sooty sockets of last year's towns, torched by Metacomet.

Liquid heat trickled down her leg; then the water spurted from her womb, pulsing and throbbing forth until it seemed that all the world's seas broke from a single bag of water, until the snow melted under her feet.

Catherwood opened her eyes. Gabriel stood watching her from the open door, a candle shining in his hand. The fisher and cat spun almost imperceptibly under bare trees, under a blazing mantle of stars.

1678

The Ax-marked Trees

The sight of white birch trees cooling in a drift of spring snow was so unexpected and lovely that Catherwood stared.

"Lost, Elisabeth," she said.

Elisabeth's hands, resting on Cath's shoulders, patted her lightly. The baby was hunched against Cath, arms outstretched and bottom pushed high in the air. She flopped her head back and forth, searching for the best spot on Cath's shoulder, then gave a sigh like a sung note.

Cath stood still and hugged the baby against her bodice. Her back ached, and an arrow of fear, a small flamy thing, darted up her spine. As chilly air off the water climbed around her, she set off again. It was only midafternoon. Surely she could find her way before nightfall. Retracing her steps, she wondered at her own carelessness. She could find no trace of an ax on any tree; this was not the path the cousins had carefully laid out, chopping a guide mark into every large tree. It must have been the ground, hard-packed like a trail, not yet fully awakened by spring, that misled. That and a sense of familiarity, a feeling of confidence in the knowledge of her feet, as if they could know a road home even in the dark. But it was not true, and she could see no recognizable shape in tree or rock or stream. A moment of forgetfulness and the world fell awry, dropped out of truth. *Gone ban twivy twist*. "And Gabriel not looking for us till tomorrow," she said aloud. Missing her husband, Cath had left Richard and Sarah's house after a morning visit.

She felt sure that if she walked east she would cross the path and catch sight of a gashed tree. She wished she had remembered to take Gabriel's precious compass from his chest.

"The compass, a box of firestones, and a

sheathed knife." Gabriel had told her always to carry those three with her in the forest. A wooden box of flints and a knife of Arab steel lay in the bottom of her sack. There was also some clean baby linen. Elisabeth's nightgown and a smock. Her own nightgown. Spare moccasins for the baby. Spare laces. Silk stockings. A pair of sea-green slippers. Two flat cakes bundled in a length of tow. A small Indian pot, Mary's gift. A doll Will had made.

Both were warmly clad, if it came to the worst and they had to sleep a night in the open. Dressed for visiting, Catherwood wore her silk-lined rose-colored wool cloak. Underneath was a heavy silk gown and quilted petticoat, now tucked up against mud, and layer after layer of warm smocks. The baby's rose velvet cloak and her loose gown and smocks resembled her mother's clothing, and both wore worsted stockings under their high leather boots.

"No," Cath said. She must find the ax-marked trees.

For an hour she walked east, the sun at her back. The baby's cloud of warm breath rhythmically moistened Cath's neck. When she woke, Elisabeth bucked against her mother's arms, struggling to get down. Cath hung on to her a minute, running toward a sunlit boulder at the edge of a stream.

"Wah-ah," said Elisabeth, holding a hand out to the stream. "Wah."

"Water," Cath said, unfastening her bodice. The baby was hungry, latching on the breast and drinking without stopping. "Ah," said Cath, leaning back in stages until she lay flat on the ground, closing her eyes as the ache in her back slowly began to disperse. It flowed down her legs and arms from a core of pain. Elisabeth shoved her face against the other breast, pushing the gown aside with her chin. Cath sank into sleep, then woke again in sharp alarm. The little girl was rooting in the sack, pulling out shoes and cloth and throwing them behind her. "Thanks be to God," Cath said, lying back down.

After she had emptied the bag, the baby rolled on her back, drawing up her legs and gnawing on a toy. Cath sat up and fed her pieces of cake, bite by bite, not wanting to lose a single crumb. Afterward she stripped the child and washed her underlinen in the icy stream. Elisabeth reveled in the chilly May air, giving the ground odd stiff-legged stamps and making short staggering runs in the patchy sunlight. Stopping short, she fumbled with her belly button, then bowed her legs slightly and, head down, watched herself urinate.

"Elisabeth is a mischief," said Cath, catching her up and rinsing her wet feet in the stream.

The baby squatted on her heels. Following the doodling progress of ants, she gripped her knees, head bent.

"Emmets, Elisabeth," said Cath, letting an ant tickle a path across her hand.

She raked together a bed of dry leaves, covering it with the skirt of her gown, her petticoat, and several smocks. She shivered a little from the cool air on her bare arms. Then she built a nest of sticks and leaves, trying over and over before she managed to set grass and dry frizzled heads of last year's clematis alight with a spark from flint and steel. "You be cross-grained stones," she said. All the same she placed them carefully back in the box, then in the bottom of her bag. She spent an hour collecting wood and dry brush, hauling fallen saplings to the fire. Capering by the fire, Elisabeth spun around, then tumbled to the ground.

"My sweet babe," Cath said.

The bonfire shot upward, licking last year's leaves into final redness, consuming a half-rotted log's slow burn of decay. Sparks and insects flew. As flames flooded the wood, Cath stacked branches close to the fire to dry. Thinking to signal their presence with plumes of smoke, she piled green boughs on the flames, but the black smoke became tangled and lost in the treetops. Elisabeth marched in her stiff gait, circling the fire, teasing Cath when her mother held out her nightgown. The baby would run toward her, arms lifted close together and palms up, fingers curled, only to laugh and dash away, then stretch out her arms again.

"My Elisabeth," Cath said, mirroring the little girl's smiles.

From head to toe there could surely be no baby more beautiful—even Cath's sore arms and back could not make her forget the pale blond curls that at fifteen months were becoming springs, the blue eyes and upturned nose, a mouth like Gabriel's with its bowed upper and sensual under lip. Lovely curving arms, dimpled hands, round tummy neatly turning under, mound and cleft, buttocks each with a tiny roll beneath, slender shapely legs, narrow feet and toes: Catherwood and Gabriel were sure no child was ever more delicate, no child ever moved in a more dazzling halo of light.

"Like something shiny slipped into your eyes," Cath had told Gabriel. "Like the glare on a Dutch tile."

But now it was only tears, swimming so that Elisabeth wavered and kicked in a smear of light. Cath wished for Gabriel, remembering the night before when they had sat twined together in the chimney seat and watched her, so proud of their child, each in love with her antic games.

"Tomorrow we be home safe."

Catherwood wiped her eyes on her smock. Her own heat would keep Elisabeth warm enough, and the cloak would have to do for a counterpane.

She caught the baby around the middle and pulled her down, wrestling the nightgown over her head. "Ma," Elisabeth protested, "Ma. Mama." Cath knotted the gown over the child's belly, leaving her half-naked. Then she draped the wet linen on boughs by the fire and lay down to watch Elisabeth dance.

"Just like at home, she is just so merry."

*   *   *

Elisabeth woke at dawn, crawling into her mother's lap to nurse. Throwing more wood on the fire, as she had done every time she waked in the night, alerted by the hooting of owls, by a high-pitched animal shriek, or by the ragged barks of foxes, Catherwood crept close to the warmth. The baby nursed eagerly but trembled with morning cold. Where it almost brushed the flames, the damp cloak wrapped around mother and child steamed unpleasantly.

Cath could not make up her mind whether to go or stay. If she continued east, she might be mistaken and leave the path farther behind. If she waited by the fire, she might be lingering while the path lay close at hand.

She would stay by the fire, Cath decided, at least until their damp clothes were entirely dry and the air a little warmer. She and Elisabeth finished the first of the hearth cakes, and Cath drank thirstily from the stream. Water seemed not so poor when there was nothing else. Blinking, putting up a hand to touch her mother's cheek or the line of her jaw, the baby slumped peacefully in her lap.

"Da," she said sleepily, "Dadada."

Cath cupped the baby's head, then stroked her cheek, whorled ear, and hair. Elisabeth grasped one of her mother's fingers with both hands. In moments, lulled by milk and the hot fire, she closed her eyes. Cath curled around her, sleepy and for the moment unafraid. When she waked she would know what to do. "Lord, deliver us," she whispered, and then sleep sifted through her bones.

After several hours Cath stirred, then abruptly sat up.

"There she is."

The baby had tugged off her dirty linen and worsted stockings. Smeared with earth on face and legs, she busily raked the ground with twigs, scratching signs and then rubbing them out. The curls on the back of her head had been rumpled in sleep and stuck out in long frizzled spines.

"All driggle-draggle with dirt."

Cath plucked the soaked linen from under a fir tree. She worked methodically, scrubbing the stockings and linen in the stream. Hung close to hot fire, the cloth hissed and smoked, drying into stiff, wrinkled shapes. Catherwood sat close by, breaking off bits of hearth cake to feed the baby. Playful,

Elisabeth squeezed her eyes shut and opened her mouth wide, so that she resembled a hungry chick. Afterward Cath picked the tangles from the child's hair, then scooped water from the stream and splashed her face clean. Muddy rivulets trickled down Elisabeth's protesting face.

"Done, my Elisabeth."

The sun strengthened in brightness and drew the chill from the air. Already Gabriel would be walking or riding toward his cousin Robert's house, intending to meet her along the way. If only she had ridden a horse yesterday! The horses knew the way between the three houses well enough. Soon Gabriel would be alarmed to find that she and Elisabeth were gone. Perhaps he would travel on to the next cousin, perhaps the families would begin to search immediately.

She would walk east, Cath decided, but no more than a mile. If she heard the sound of shots or a hail, she would call out and drum with a rock on stone, light a green fire. She didn't allow herself to think about alternatives, didn't think beyond the next day. Would not let herself kindle with that small and flamy arrow of fear. She would search for a sheltered spot to rest in case they must sleep out one more night. "More ill night airs," she said aloud, "more damp." Elisabeth could eat hearth cake, and she would eat what remained. They would be found before a day passed.

Lost

Torquelike, fear encircled her throat with its dull, constant pressure. On their seventh day in the forest, Catherwood could no longer believe that Gabriel would find them, or that she would discover herself on the doorstep of home. For six days she had wandered in circles, trying to cross the path. Once she had dreamed someone fired a fowling piece in the woods, but she had waked to nothing but the whistles of birds. Once she closed her eyes and said, "We be back at Grevel House with Jamie chasing a painted ball and Lacey reading aloud to Mother. And we be there too, picking bloody warriors to weave a crown." Elisabeth's fingers fluttered on her eyelids. "Ma," she said, "way up." When Cath opened her eyes there was Elisabeth and the big wilderness of America. "A mizmaze, Elisabeth." Certain only that she was west of Albany, she began to walk northeast, toward the river. She would meet a trapper or a party from Fort Orange or a band of the River Indians, the Mahicans.

The fear was always there, hands around her neck, for Elisabeth needed clean clothes, cooked food, a warm bed at night. On the seventh morning, Catherwood's milk took minutes to let down, and she worried that they were moving too quickly. She decided they would walk only from dawn until noon. The rest of the day she could wash soiled linen, collect wood and nurse last night's carefully preserved coals into new fire, prepare food, and weave a shelter of hurdles. Sarah's gift of a clay pot had been a lucky providence, and Cath could not think how else she could have carried coals from camp to camp. Flints were frustrating, hard to use.

So far they were not starved, although Cath always felt hungry. *Thank God for*

Mother Childe, she thought. She had loved going to visit the old woman, poking about her house, learning about plants. The cottage seemed no more than a thatched nest, the outer walls and roof greening with moss, so that even the very quarrels in the one window by the door were layered with a thinnest green. Mother Childe reminded Cath of a hedgehog with her gnarled and humped back, her bristly mustache, her prickly wool cloak starred with burrs and seeds, and bits of withered flowers stuck in the shock of strawlike hair, part hanging down her back, part stacked loosely on top of her head. The principal beauty of her youth lingered: bold eyes like blue stones, looking out of a labyrinth of wrinkles.

Fearless, curious, Cath trailed Mother Childe as she scurried, rooting through sacks and bowls for medicines. For Margarett's brother who gasped and choked and could not catch his breath, there was a parcel of thorn-apple leaves to be steeped in wine with sage and strawberry leaves. Periwinkle for Gaffer Withycombe's toothache. Balm and feverfew in ale for Gaffer Tap's boneshave. Then there was Mrs. Grevel's usual potion, made with wine and stored in clay bottles. "Lavender water," Mother Childe told the girl, "pepper for the blood flow, dried lily-of-the-valley roots and flowers, good for apoplexy, distilled in wine for six weeks."

Between what she had learned from herb-women and from others at Grevel House, Cath recognized many herbs and plants, some of which she knew by name. She tasted others that looked edible, looked like cousins to the plants of home, spitting out any too bitter leaf. Plants were frightening because they became curious toys to the baby, who wanted to explore their new shapes with her mouth, and Cath feared she might pick a poisonous leaf or flower, mushroom or berry. And Catherwood had another terror: that she might poison herself and die. Whenever the thought came to her, she pictured a different loss: a hungry and cold Elisabeth, tugging at her mother's bodice; an Elisabeth pawed by bears, dragged to a lair; an Elisabeth stumbling deep into the woods, falling in a ravine. Perhaps a trapper or an Indian would find the child. Or perhaps the unicorns would bear her away.

Catherwood had started foraging on the third day, eating the flower heads and heart leaves of violets, carefully avoiding bird-foot leaves for fear of monkshood and larkspur. At first Elisabeth had thrust out her tongue, refusing to eat the flowers, but Cath tore them to pieces, feeding her bit by bit. When they clung to her lips, Cath pushed the sodden petals back in her mouth.

"This is a mighty task," she said, rubbing a cheek against the baby's tangled hair.

The flowers, white and blue and purple, glimmered on a shady stream bank. How many flowers would be enough to content a baby, Cath wondered.

The baby accepted young leaves of marsh marigold and bladder campion, but the wood sorrels made her shake her head.

"Nonono," she called.

It was the close of the season for fiddleheads, and Cath collected the silvery claws of bracken, rubbing off their woolly coats. Even better were the tightly furled croziers of what the Pasturels called feather fern, a brilliant green under papery scales. Violets and young ferns were already plentiful along streams and in the moist woods, and once she came on a patch of morels.

Cath shaped cooking pots from the bark of paper birches, the seams patched with pine resin. The first efforts were leafy cones; with practice she fashioned a crude bucket. After she sealed the pots, cooking was simple—when they didn't break apart or spill under the pressures of cooking. Using a makeshift shovel of bark, Cath scooped rocks from the bed of coals and tipped them into a stew of leaves, stems, and roots.

It was good to give thanks, to eat, to make a bonfire to frighten away animals and provide warmth, to weave a shelter of branches and willow withies. Still, the grasp of fear never left her throat, and her longing for Gabriel was so palpable that she believed he must feel the yearnings of her heart, concentrated on him and Elisabeth. For these two only could keep her alive, keep her digging roots in the muck or heaping up waste wood to burn, weaving a shelter in the spring rain.

The Seventeenth Day

On the seventeenth day Catherwood and the baby explored the banks of a river. Cath began to doubt herself, unsure whether this was Henry Hudson's river. Attempting to follow the river north, she found that the banks seemed to point her toward the setting sun. She could recall no large river flooding into the Hudson, but until now she had imagined herself to be west and most probably southwest of Albany. For several miles she continued to walk, until she wept from vexation and from the pain in her back. She wondered whether she might pass between settlements and reach an unknown territory.

After a night's sleep, she decided to travel in one direction, not to wander or circle about the forests. In that way she would be most likely to cross a path. She could not hope to walk all the way to the coast, where she might easily find a town; she wanted to go north, where there must be many trading posts and forts. But the nameless river flowing from west to east cut her off from the forests to the north.

The next day, while foraging for food, Cath encountered the first people she had seen since she became lost. She was tired and held Elisabeth by the hand, letting her weave and stop to pick up leaves and pebbles. Cath spotted some heathlike plants at the margin of a bog but found nothing to eat. Chewing slowly on a leaf, she followed the edge of a pool. Her boots squelched in the damp ground, and she lifted the baby to her hip, passing through a grove of tamaracks and black spruce. Just beyond the rim of trees, a group of children played—boys of three and four dressed in miniature hunting shirts and leggings, a girl in a short dress and leggings. Cath gasped, stepping back, but Elisabeth eagerly held out her hands. "See chiller," she called. Where the ground became bog, two women paused in their work and looked up, exchanging a quiet glance. There were no men in the group, and Cath saw that one of the women packed an infant on her back, the baby wrapped in skins and lashed to a board. Another baby lay sleeping in a bundle of skins.

"The river?" she asked, pointing north. "Henry Hudson's river?"

The women looked at each other, then one shook her head, responding in her own language.

"I," Cath said, tapping her breast, "want to go home with you." She gestured at them, then walked her fingers up her arm.

The younger woman coughed and spat. Did she understand? Cath touched three fingers in turn, then indicated herself and the other two. She knelt and made the three fingers glide through the low heath plants. The fingers came to rest on the curve of her other hand.

"We can go," she said. "We three can go to your village."

The younger woman spoke loudly, shaking her head. The syllables jostled against Cath's ear, stranger than any language she knew.

"You speak English? English?" she asked, turning to the other.

The older woman jerked her head to one side, as though listening.

"She don't speak English," Cath told the baby. "Bad luck for us, Elisabeth."

The younger woman continued raking sphagnum from the bog, tearing off the edges of an immense floating mat. With a short bone knife she cut the dense carpet into pieces.

Cath pointed to the drifting island, mingled red and green, then to her mouth.

"Eat?"

The two women bent over, shouting with laughter so that the children sprinted back to the shore. The younger woman spoke to them, and they laughed shrilly, bounding and racing in circles. Elisabeth jumped and struggled in her mother's arms; uncertain, Cath put her down and let her totter after the others.

The older woman cried out, following the baby to touch her pale curls, making admiring noises. Elisabeth held her hands out, palms up, and the woman knelt beside her. They chattered together, one speaking in babble, the other in her own language. *Surely Mahican, not Mohawk*, Cath thought.

The children gathered around, tugging at Elisabeth's gown. Making short runs at them, the baby grabbed their deerskin clothes, thudded to the ground when they backed away. Cath's hand grazed a child's head, the matt sheen of shoulder-length hair. "Beautiful," she said, nodding at the mothers. Her face felt tight and unmoving, engraved with a small smile.

The girl pretended to wolf some moss, and the family collapsed into laughter. The older woman uncauled her baby, showing Cath the sphagnum diapering the child's bottom.

Cath laughed, her voice wavering. The woman gave her a dripping length of moss, pointing from the moss to Elisabeth, who staggered after the older children, laughing with the wild shrieks that Gabriel called her fairy laughter.

"Thank you." Cath nodded.

The younger woman called sharply to the younger children. When she approached, Cath stepped back. The woman's strong hand rested for an instant on Elisabeth's hair, then twisted the curls around her fingers.

"Ma. Mama," Elisabeth called.

"Ah," cried Cath, reaching for the child, kneeling on the ground.

The young woman still grasped the bone knife in her other hand. The tip was sharp like an arrow. There was a harsh metallic taste in Cath's mouth. She looked quickly from one woman to the other. Were these the Mahicans, the peaceful people called the River Indians by the English? Dizzy, she gripped the baby, but Elisabeth bucked in her arms.

If only she could cross the river! At Fort Orange she had heard a trapper complain that the northern woods were too crowded for him. So many trappers and soldiers, a man could find no elbow room.

Afraid to show alarm, she let go the baby's wrist, and Elisabeth pushed off from her mother's skirts. Cath's hand slipped to her throat as the older woman's eyes fastened on her gold necklace. It was one worn by her mother when she died, but when Cath saw the woman's interest, she unlatched the chain and held the pendant in the palm of her hand.

She gestured to herself and Elisabeth, then to the women. "Indian camp," she said, over and over. Again she walked her fingers to a village of leaves; again the younger woman shook her head. Cath could see only two choices. She could trail these women to a camp, whether peaceful or fierce she could not know. Or she could make another bargain with them.

Cath hesitated, thinking of the younger woman's fingers wound in Elisabeth's hair, the bone knife close to her daughter's soft face. Then she pointed in the direction of the river. The two women watched as Cath plucked a leaf. This time she pointed from herself and the baby to a twig which she broke and placed on the leaf. The younger woman went back to tearing lengths of moss, but the elder watched intently. Cath motioned for her to come closer and placed the leaf at the water's edge, pushing the leaf boat across the surface. "River," she said, rippling the water with a hand while lifting the boat across with the other. "To cross the water." Again she pointed toward the river.

The woman made a single decisive nod as she accepted the necklace.

So Catherwood returned to the riverbank.

She and the older woman walked east along the shore, one child asleep in Cath's arms, another slumbering on a cradleboard. Now that she had a chance of meeting a party of Indians, Catherwood was afraid, not of this woman with her homely concerns, but of the tribe, the warriors. Soon, in the northern woods, she would find what she hoped to be coarse but well-meaning men who spoke her own language. But then again, this woman was near, able to help, and northern trappers might not be as plentiful as in the Fort Orange man's boasts. Cath remembered the bone knife, the fingers knotted in Elisabeth's hair. What had it meant—a threat, promise, an idle act? Mohawk or Mahican? *Just crabbed and crankety, maybe.* Why should a woman of the woods be any less subject to moods and whims than a woman of towns? Perhaps she should hold fast to what lay here before her: another human being, who knew the forest and streams better than she.

Her companion halted by a thicket, groping in the dense foliage. Cath knelt, glimpsing an awkward boat of elm bark. Again the woman reached into the brush, this time drawing out a shapely birchbark canoe.

"Indian camp?" Cath asked once more. The only response was an unreadable look, then a headshake. The older woman pushed the boat across the grass and onto the mud and rock at the river's edge. The canoe bobbed on the water, lurching only when Cath gathered up her gown and climbed inside.

The woman paddled without pause, glancing up at the overcast sky as the canoe shot over the waves. It was cold on the water, and Cath sheltered the baby under her cloak. Elisabeth's head popped out, staring quietly at the water. *Was crossing the river a right step*, wondered Cath. *If not, I do not know one morsel bit how to go.* Perhaps she should have tried to barter the necklace for a canoe, although she had sailed in a boat only three times in her life. Streams and rivers in York could be wild and whimsical, drowning a boat in play. Perhaps she should have dogged the women and children until they drove her back with stones. Or let her stay. The canoe scudded slantwise across the river, slapped and thumped by waves. In midstream Cath gave over worrying about her choice, letting her thoughts dissolve. For a few minutes she dozed, the baby's plump cheek pressed to hers. Then the canoe grated on stones and shells, and Cath stood on shore, her cloak heavy and damp. *Flisked with water.* The necklace, its gold warm against skin—Mahican or Mohawk—gleamed in the early afternoon light.

"Mother," Cath said. "If Mother knew."

For an instant she was far away, remembering in one fell swoop the day Lacey had unfastened the chain from Elisabeth Grevel's neck.

That afternoon Elisabeth and Cath walked far into the park despite a cold wind, wandering out to where Gaffer Withycombe and Henry Pasturel were finishing the winter pruning of apple trees, then back to the shrubbery paths. Cath urged her mother to return to the house, but Elisabeth delayed, exhilarated by the wind and by the clouds that scudded across the smoldering brand of winter sun.

The two women stopped in the shelter of a hedgerow, huddling close together in their red cloaks, talking about Gabriel Lyte.

"I would not force my daughter's mind, but three months be flown by, and soon he will be asking for a reply."

Cath looked across the evergreen walk,

furling her cloak more tightly around her body. Rivulets of air seeped through the hedge, pressing against the heavy camlet.

Gabriel Lyte. When she and Gabriel Lyte crossed the green fields at Glastonbury, momentarily alone save for the broken molars of the abbey jutting within the curve of the town, she had promised to think about him, to consider the New World before him, and although she felt nearly certain that she could not leave her mother, it was a vow and a duty she took some pleasure in. Once she had been a barefoot beggar child, and now in her own right she held a marriage portion and the power to choose. "I will choose this very day," she told Elisabeth, "if you be content to walk in."

"It is bitter." Elisabeth hesitated a moment longer. "I would not have thee go far from me; yet would not have thee miss so fair a chance. Mr. Lyte is of the gentry, one who can rightly wear a sword, one with some Oxford learning. But more important is his seeming kindness. He was not brought to hate those unlike himself in faith or country; nor to appear careless of a woman's heart, nor neglectful of honor."

Cath linked her arm with her mother's,

gently steering her toward the house. "And this the first you spoke of it."

"I would not choose for another."

In the parlor Elisabeth, chilled and white around the mouth, knelt by the fire. Margarett brought them wine and lily water. The day wound down with its quiet duties, some household sewing, prayers. Cath stayed up after Elisabeth went to bed, crouched by the fireplace, wrapped in a thick bed rug, and thought about Gabriel Lyte and the New World.

She remembered the strength in Gabriel Lyte's arms, lifting her lightly from the stone wall below the orchard, the start of fear she felt, as though she might drop a long way in his arms. There would be no stone walls in the New World, just league after league of woods and swamp and wild river. But it was a mother's arms she remembered most, the hours Elisabeth spent holding and rocking her, as if she could rock away all the lost girl's unhappiness and uncertainty. Her mother had taught her how to read and to write, how to sew, plain and fine; how to play the harpsichord and to sing. She had showed her how to be modest and mannerly, softening the child's rough ways until she was almost another being from the lice-ridden and bruised girl who stumbled headlong into a new life. *Mine, mine* called the child's voice, rising from the frozen muck, ringing in memory.

Late in the evening Catherwood threw off the rug, moved to the bedroom with her candle.

Moonlight filtered onto the bed curtains. Inside, Elisabeth Grevel and Ursula and Margarett would be long asleep, Margarett pushed to the outermost edge because Ursula complained that green girls bucked and kicked in their dreams. Quickly Catherwood undressed, draping her clothes over the back of a bench, pulling on a gown. In the dark her foot grazed a shard that skittered across the boards. She held the candle low to the floor and saw a curve of glass joined to a heavy ball and foot: one of Elisabeth's precious goblets, broken.

"Mother?" There was a sweet odor of lilies steeped in wine. "Mother?"

She tripped over a fallen bolster, catching herself on the bed curtains. Lifting the candle, she pulled back the curtain and saw that Elisabeth lay twisted, her head tipped over the edge of the bed. Catherwood's attention was gripped by her mother's raised hand, the outstretched fingers tangled in chain, the gold and amethyst flower pressing into her forefinger, so that a bead of blood clung to one of the four petals. In the shimmering candlelight her face resembled a mask, the mouth open and set irregularly with teeth like blue stone, the eyes dull gray stone. Catherwood saw but waited, delayed the knowing with her candle lifted in the air— and then her voice rose to a high, unwearied keening.

For Elisabeth would never see the costards bloom again, or gather summer herbs to strew, or leave morning footprints on the leavings of a white frost. Nothing remained anywhere on earth for Elisabeth Grevel. Not even knowing that Cath had stayed up late, determining, deciding irrevocably, that she could not marry Gabriel Lyte despite his black hair and the blue eyes that caught and held her gaze, despite the grip of his hand that made her start and tremble when he helped her over the icy stones in the stream below the house, despite his alluring stories of a new world.

Elisabeth would never know! Never know that she had given up the man and the lovely, alarming territory in her imagination. That she would renounce them a thousand times, that there was no home for Catherwood but the one she had found with Elisabeth.

The memory swept down on her like a bird, alighting for one vivid instant, then flying on.

Now the Indian woman thrust the canoe forward in the water, leaping into the stern and shouting out something that might have been a farewell. The child on her back gazed at Cath and Elisabeth without blinking.

"Wait," Cath called once, then said "No." The canoe moved rhythmically on, and only the baby strapped to the cradleboard looked back. Catherwood's choice was made.

"Not glad," Cath whispered.

"Boat, wah."

"Boat, water," Cath repeated.

"I be all on end," she said, kneeling down to embrace her daughter.

The canoe shrank small as a leaf on water before Catherwood faced north, throwing the sack over her shoulder and hoisting Elisabeth back to her hip.

A Steel Knife

The most precious thing Catherwood owned was the knife, not an iron knife but one with a Damascus-steel blade and a metal handle curiously engraved with arabesque vines and birds. Her hand knew its shape, its pressure, and the nick where blade flowed into haft. The knife peeled the stalks of cattail and sweetflag, skinned a chipmunk, slit the throats of baby mice sheltered under a rotted log, severed the shell of a turtle, speared grubs from their larval lairs. The knife always reminded her of Gabriel, the one who had thought it right to place the very keenest blade in her sack.

On her twentieth day in the wilderness, Cath made good use of the knife. The morning's walk finished, Cath sat cross-legged on the ground, dressed in a smock, nightgown, and cloak. The baby had been listless for several days but now Elisabeth was nursing, almost asleep, and in a moment her head rolled to one side. Her cheeks were red with warmth, and her full underlip shone with milk. Cath lifted the baby onto a bed of leaves and covered her with the small cloak. Although it was the start of June, the air remained chilly.

Eyes shut, chin lifted so that the sun fell full on her face, Cath heard a distant flurry of wings. A few minutes later she saw a flock of a thousand birds flying high overhead; then suddenly and swiftly, as though freed from a vast cage, the numbers and noise swelled until a great cataract of wings battered the air. An avalanche tilted sideways by a large ruthless hand, the torrent of birds blotted out the sun so that Cath trembled, kneeling over the baby in unexpected twilight. The passionate tumult rippled, veered, and spilled down staircases of air, shot at high speed to the forest canopy. An astonishing, troubling sight: Cath stared up as the black watercourse cascaded, plummeting and peeling off into a thousand millraces and flumes like water falling artlessly through air, tumbling through each cranny and glade. Birds thumped to the ground, beating a wing to right themselves, graceless as chickens trussed in a tow sack. Flecks of noise spattered the trees, resolved into a startled chortling and cooing in the branches. Feathers and down, half-digested grain and berries rained on Cath and Elisabeth, who woke and half stood with hands on knees, shrieking soundlessly with open mouth. Cath started up, seized a chunk of wood, and clubbed the newly fallen birds. They continued to leak through the branches, dropping awkwardly to the ground. She knocked more birds off the trees, jabbing at boughs studded with birds. Stunned, unable to flutter up, they waddled drunkenly on the forest floor.

A fierce desire swept through Cath, a desire fed by the unappeased and openmouthed face of Elisabeth. They would live, they would live and grow strong on the fat birds. She harried them with a stick, without pity for the plump fleeing bodies that wobbled through the grass and last year's leaves. Chattering and singing, a ribbon of birds rose and hovered in the air, and then a great pour of wings streamed into the abyss of heaven. Below the rushing sound of ribbon after ribbon unreeling into air, Elisabeth's screams became faintly audible. Cath shook low branches, striking the last birds with such force that their limp bodies flew across the grass one final time. At last she dropped to her knees, gasping from exertion.

"Birds, Elisabeth, sweet turtledoves," she called, stepping across the birds, some jerking, some ruffled but still.

The baby cried shamelessly, red-faced, tears and mucus glazing her chin and cheeks. She held up her cupped hands, and Catherwood swung her into place, head snuggled against her mother's neck, the child body snuggled against her own curves.

"A wonder, how she cuddles in and fits me," Cath said, her face soaked with Elisabeth's tears, "like she is made there forever."

She remembered how Gammer Withycombe had coaxed little children. *I would'n cry, I would'n cry, there's a little maid, a little man, no, I would'n.* In a moment Cath began singing a song to Elisabeth, a song nothing like a bird's song, while wounded birds flapped and crawled around her.

That afternoon Catherwood raddled a sturdy shelter from brush and stakes and lit a bonfire in an opening between trees. She did not want to lose a single bird to foxes or to other, larger, animals. All afternoon and into the night she cleaned and gutted birds, throwing entrails into the fire. The pigeons were lovely, with backs of soft gray and dun tipped with black, some with pale rusty breasts and feet. Cath roasted five birds on a spit, tearing off bits of meat for the baby, who sucked on them greedily and then opened her mouth for more. "Mo," she said, "mo." For the first time since she became lost, Cath dropped asleep without hunger pains. At dawn she continued, cutting thin slices of meat to dry on racks of sticks by the fire.

She planned to stay by the fire in the clearing for up to five days, drying meat and gleaning food from the nearby brook. On the third day she had another piece of good luck while gathering wood. That morning it rained, soaking some of the meat. In the afternoon she threw her remaining wood on the fire and set out for more, carrying Elisabeth on her hip. When she spotted dry brush and fallen limbs, she let the baby play with twigs and stones while she dragged kindling and timber into heaps. During the long labor of hauling the wood back to the fire, the baby's weight still on her hip, a whitetail flashed from a stand of briers and scudded away. Curious, Cath approached and saw that the doe's fawn lay behind a tangle of thorns and leaves in a fresh pool, his white markings spangling the rainwater. The fawn held his head poised, and his eyes gleamed; a heartbeat ticked at his throat. When Elisabeth made a small cry of pleasure, Cath clutched her tightly. She must slaughter the fawn—she would never have a chance at a deer, the meat and skin both so needful, and she might never stumble upon another. Her hands were small, and Cath feared she could not throttle the animal, even young as it was. The steel knife lay cold in her bodice. She set the baby on the ground, bringing her a quartz stone, a handful of violets, and some fir cones.

"Stay," she said, "stay," pushing the child back down when she tried to rise.

Stripping off her cloak, Cath knelt by the

thorns. The fawn still gleamed in the pool. All her life she had seen animals die, had helped with or overseen the butchering of meat for winter, but until now she had never killed anything larger than a chicken. She wiped her hands on her nightgown. With dried meat from the birds and deer, she could remain strong to carry Elisabeth what might be many miles to a settlement or trading post. How hungry she had been until now, traipsing up and down the rolling countryside, bearing the baby on her hip. *I must*, Cath thought. There would be meat, organs, broth, marrow, spotted hide. The lustrous eyes drank in the gloom under the thorns, darkening as if to collect all the shadows in the world's wood. She plunged to her knees, pinning the little creature's head to the ground. He half staggered up, his hooves scrabbling for purchase on the moist earth and slippery leaves. He bleated like a lamb. One dark eye shone at her as Cath pressed with all her force on the head and shoulders; still kneeling directly on the small, struggling animal, she grasped the throat and slit fur and flesh, then pushed deeper as the fawn kicked and thrashed. Red spittle foamed at his lips and blurred the bleating cries. Blood spurted over her hands, squirting between her fingers and flinging trails of red over her face and breasts. The legs churned slow, slower, paused, then made a soft pawing motion. Cath cried out, feeling the uneven pulse of blood under her hands. Her face was damp and cold, the taste of blood in her mouth. The fawn lay with his flayed neck open in the gloom, only the beauty of his coat remaining to him, a dead unrippling light on leaves. Rinsing her face and hands in the rosy water of the pool, Cath remembered the doe, swerving between trees.

"Mama. Ma," Elisabeth called. The baby stood leaning as though about to tumble forward, a fir cone in her outstretched hand.

The dead fawn's head drooped on its stalk, and the pool of water shook with rosy stars.

Summer in
the Northern Hills

Cath husked the bloom spikes of cattails, dropping them into a crude bucket. They would eat when Elisabeth woke, but now she lay limp in Cath's lap, releasing a few faint cries but seldom stirring. She was dressed warmly, underneath wearing the diaper of deerskin that Cath had scraped free of hair and softened with the fawn's own brains. Inside lay a strip of sphagnum moss, absorbent and antiseptic. The day before, an insect had crept inside Elisabeth's gown and bitten her on the legs and thighs, leaving red welts with tiny jaw marks at their center. Frightened by the trail of bites, Cath had quickly built a shelter and a fire to warm the baby. She had stayed awake until morning, the baby lying slack in her arms. At dawn the fever sank, and Elisabeth felt well enough to sit up and nuzzle against her mother. Alarmed that the baby had gone without eating for a day, Cath spent the morning foraging, circling the fire where Elisabeth slept, homing to the smoke every few minutes to check on Elisabeth and to pile wood and green branches on the flames. Smoke was her safety signal, for she feared becoming lost again—becoming lost from her child. She gathered a meal of cattail shoots and pollen, greenbrier shoots, and mint leaves with wild rose petals for tea. Some of her precious strips of dried meat soaked in hot water.

Cath lay down beside the baby, stroking her cheek and smelling the sweetness of her hair. Two mornings back she had spotted a mass of soapwort blossoms—immigrants colonizing the remains of a collapsed hut—and spent the day scrubbing their clothes with the crushed plants. Cath had bathed in a cold stream but warmed water for the baby's bath. When she woke again, Cath would feed her the buds from cattail shoots, tucking the grains into her mouth one by one.

Weeks in the wood had taught Cath that she and Elisabeth could survive, if they remained healthy and free from accidents. Each day she felt stronger, could walk farther carrying her sack, with Elisabeth riding on her shoulders or astride her hip. Hunger kept pace with her, and in her back was a dull wearying pain. But her arms and legs strengthened, so she could walk for almost a mile without putting the baby down. Yet however muscular and lean she became, fear still clasped her throat. She feared the chill in summer mornings and nights, feared each new plant she tasted, feared that she might drift aimlessly between settlements and into uncharted wilderness. Only when she knelt by the fire with a healthy Elisabeth slumbering in her arms, her prayers told, did Cath fear nothing. The universe at her back seemed to allow her shelter and warm space, the sun and worn moon by day and moon and stars by night shining down as though mother and child were the peaceful swaying center of the world.

"Dadada," Elisabeth would say, no longer questioning. "Da house." Cath liked to think that the baby dreamed of Gabriel, recalling him with less home-sickness than at first.

Catherwood felt a certainty that her link to Gabriel held unbroken, that he would not give up hope and release her to the wilderness, that a spun thread joined them. A silk thread rambling through the forests of North America, unreeling and constant, though impossible as a guide home. She needed no glance from his blue eyes, no perfect memory of his profile and black hair to feel his strength and endurance. *An untoppled English tower. Strong sleave-silk. The basal leaves of cattails, malleable until twisted into rushing, cords that last a hundred, maybe a thousand years.*

Cath and the baby lingered at the camp near the marsh for a week, until Elisabeth appeared fit and happy again. The red blots on her legs slowly faded, but hard lumps remained, one as large as a robin's egg. For three more days they camped in a burned-over meadow, feeding on wild strawberries. Elisabeth walked stiff-legged through the field, squatting to pick the berries and sometimes eating them cap and all. When days turned warm, Cath let her go naked in the afternoons. On the third day a light rain fell, glistening in the strawberry leaves, and Cath killed and roasted a spruce grouse with its chick.

"Silly birds," Cath said. Will had caught spruce grouse the year before, letting them waddle into a baited sack or grabbing one with both hands.

These were sipping water from the leaves, or perhaps eating the berries. The mother feigned a broken wing, scrambling away from the baby, but Cath snatched up the bird and wrung its neck. She let Elisabeth hold the chick, which sat still and quiet in the grass.

"Waiting for a mother to come," Cath said. "But she ban't coming."

The frightened bird fluttered under Elisabeth's clutch, releasing a single red dew drop on her palm. The little girl leaned over and set the bird down gently, then squatted to watch it trundle under the strawberry leaves. When the wings fluttered she poked the bird with a finger, and the chick settled down, feathers puffed.

"Pretending to be a leaf." Cath knelt on the ground.

"Ma. Birt."

"Bird," Cath repeated. "Poor small one."

When Cath slipped the chick away and pinched its neck, Elisabeth was bewildered. Cath had been careful not to take the bird from the baby's hand, fearing that she would fling herself on the ground, crying and banging her forehead as she had done that morning when Cath unclenched a strange berry from her fist. Lately it seemed that she wept easily. For many minutes afterward Elisabeth searched, calling "Birbirbir" and staring intently at the leaves. By the fire she discovered the tuft of feathers that had been the chick, the beak drooped in defeat, the crimped claws, the shut eye like a buttonhole on an infant's gown. "Birt fall down," she said. Elisabeth turned the wad in her hands, then let it drop.

The next morning Cath packed at dawn, carrying her sack and dried meat and berries in a basket woven from cattail leaves. It fit snug to her back, with wide flat handles that circled under her arms and over her shoulders. Cath worried about their slow pace, for they had walked only a few days between the river and the camp where she had killed the pigeons. Afterward she had stopped to cure meat, to nurse Elisabeth, to wash clothes and bathe, to pick berries. Having crossed the river on the third of June, she now calculated the date as the twenty-fourth. Only five days' good travel out of so many!

She wished she had been more curious about the rivers and lakes of New York, about the forts and trading posts. They had sounded so plentiful, so close-set in the forest. She knew there were huge lakes to the north and east. One hung like a dipper roughly north of their own settlement. But she knew that countless lakes and creeks were scattered farther to the north, waterways like a labyrinth dotted with minotaurs—the home of bears, wildcats, and wolves trickling through trees, wary of fire.

For four days Cath lost herself in hills and low mountains, and on the fifth she came to the shore of a lake, mounded with beaver lodges and so big that she could not determine its shape or size. She began walking along the shore, hoping to find a post, foraging for berries. For days she saw no sign of road or fort, traveling northeast along the edge of the lake, hills and low mountains rising in every direction. It was often cool in the mountains, but Cath and Elisabeth thrived, the baby becoming playful and boisterous again. The weight of fear lightened, for in the creeks and woods were fruits and burgeoning stalks, freshwater lobsters as big as a man's hand, and trout that Cath trapped by hammering a V of stakes into the stream bed. Funneled into the narrow gap, speckled trout or bright gillies thrashed in a woven trap, to be stuffed with mint and roasted, laid on a bed of leaves next to mid-summer roots and berries.

When Cath waded in the cold water, Elisabeth bounced by the edge of streams, half squatting, waving her arms. In shallow water Cath dredged up the roots of arrowleaf, digging into the mud around the plants with a staff. The baby loved to see the tubers, some small as beads and a few larger than a hen's egg, when they bobbed to the surface and floated away, still tethered to runners. Opening and shutting one hand expressively, she babbled as her mother plowed the mud. Once they had shared a fast-running stream with an otter who paddled and swirled onto his back, where he lay fretting a necklace of roots.

They camped near the lake's border, on

a few warm nights building a fire so close to the water that its flames shone in broken shards on the low waves. "Cockles, Elisabeth," Cath said, pointing to the wind-blown ripples. The fresh air skated across the world and across the lake, sinking them in dreamless slumber. At dawn Cath drank from the cold lake, then warmed water with mint leaves while she sat crosslegged by the fire and night drained from the air.

Standing on the shore of a lake so large it would take many days to be mapped and understood, Cath felt a stray happiness. She knew the thread binding them to home held unbroken. *Gabriel.* On her cloak lay Elisabeth, healthy, stained with berries. The sun dusted every crook and cranny of the landscape, and the world shone. Hope rose up, springing like a lake's source out from rock. In forest and creek the abundance of early July encircled mother and child like a promise, for despite all, they had survived to the season of plenty. Cath remembered the lilies of the field, dressed more finely than Solomon in all his glory. Her spirit surged and poured, as fluent as the vast flocks of North American birds, as swerving as any stream.

A Trapper

Laughing, Elisabeth marched off a boulder into air and into her mother's arms. It was a game she had played for many months, since before they were lost, when she would jump off a low chest or clamber up on the table of trestles and boards. Never in her short life had her mother or Gabriel failed to catch the baby and swing her up to their arms, down to the earth, or outward in an arc that made her shriek. Dizzy with pleasure, she dropped down, belly to the earth, cocking her lower legs up and patting the ground with both hands. Moments later she squatted, then launched herself forward, scaling the rock again.

As they wandered along the lake and hills, Cath reveled in the baby's merriment and good health. The last welts with their hard kernels faded from her legs. They stopped to play on the shore, launching bark ships masted with sticks and hung with leafy sails. Elisabeth rocked stiff-legged on pebbles, danced and tossed her arms. Morning and night she liked to tease, jerking the emptied carry basket over her face, butting it off again as she shouted, "Eye peep, eye peep." Any fallen piece of cloth or smock became a prop for games. "Takee. Hide," she called, bringing her wooden doll to Cath with both hands. The old places were always best to Elisabeth, always the ones that made her shout with the glee of finding: in the sack, in the basket, inside a cloak.

During the easy days of short walks and abundant food, Cath's milk came in more strongly, and there was more chance for rest. Mother and baby dozed by the fire in the afternoon, content and warm. It was as close to an idyll as constant foraging, travel over rough ground, and the daily making of shelter could be. To Cath the days appeared sweet because each held constant in its supply of food and good weather.

One day in July she discovered a single hatchet mark on a tree and, close by, a pit trap baited with a paste of rotted fish and covered with fir branches. Panicked, elated, Cath snatched up the baby. The rest of the morning she used a rude staff, prodding leaves and scrub in her path, searching for more signs of trappers. After many days, to be so close to safety; but Cath found no other mark that morning.

Then in early afternoon, just as she was deciding to give up the day's hunt, she walked into a trapper's camp. She gripped the baby tightly, glancing from a dead fire to a splint basket and stretched deerskin to the man's length rolled in a wool blanket. The lumpy shape had made no answer to her cry of surprise, echoing on the nearby lake. Hoping for a savior, she found the mundane—a birchbark bowl of gray slurry, gobbets of meat glued to a skillet. "Orts," she said aloud. She stepped closer, hugging the baby against her breasts as if for protection. She called to him, once, twice, three times: nothing. Hair spilled in oily strands from the caul of blanket. Now the pulse in her ears slowed; now Cath could hear a man's breathing, a clammy sound. He stank. *Rammish*, Cath thought.

She hesitated, not wanting to wake him, then suddenly fearing to draw back the blanket. What if he were ill with a pestilence, with smallpox or an ague that would sweep through them both? He had failed to add wood to the fire, perhaps for a day or more, and animal tracks looped close to his feet. Perhaps he had been gnawed by foxes, she thought, kneeling to check the prints. Cath picked up a fallen branch, sliding the stick under the blanket.

"Heavy," she whispered.

"Down," Elisabeth said, pushing with her knees.

"No down, Elisabeth. No."

She fished under the blanket until the branch snagged on threads, and then she peeled the wool back from his face. The man under the blanket was young, with sharp features and a heavy beard. His long beard reeled in a tangled drunkard's path across the coarse fabric. "All-a-knickled up, Elisabeth," Cath said, "all nickle-nackle." The eyes were closed, the lips parted, and a flush tinted the face and bare chest. Cath thrust the blanket aside, exposing his belly and arms, and breathed in with a faint hissing sound that made Elisabeth reach up and lay a finger on her mother's lower lip.

It was not smallpox, nor contagion of any kind, she thought, although fright glittered when she saw the buboes under his arm. One limb lay a castaway on the dirt, alien to the rest of the man's body. Cath squatted on her heels, one knee pressed against the ground. The hand seemed the worst, with its fingers swollen and spread. Red as rose petals, Cath thought. Not pestilence but poison. A darker red streaked the red arm, and the whole man appeared flushed and hot.

"I pray you live," Cath whispered. The trapper's eyelids remained shut.

"Ah," she said. A fatal nick, a slit on the tip of his forefinger, burned deep red, its edges fretted by rot.

Elisabeth climbed down between her mother's knees, but Cath gripped her firmly, unwilling to let her explore the camp.

After Cath had tucked the blanket around the trapper, her next concern was to find out any possible sources of poison. The man's few belongings were strewn haphazardly on the ground. After wrapping fresh leaves around the haft, she gingerly picked up a knife and thrust the blade in the earth over and over. She cleaned a hatchet with earth, then carefully placed knife and hatchet in the fast-running water of a nearby stream. The year before, Gabriel had shown her how trappers could chop a hole in a beaver dam and set a trap inside the animal's own house. But this man had no pelts, at least not at this camp, only a partially cured deer-skin. Rifling through his splint pack, Cath discovered some string, a torn and greasy hat of bobcat fur, a short iron bludgeon. Not much else: the skillet, a clay pot and stopper stinking of fish, scattered parts of a bow drill, a leather hunting shirt and a torn wool shirt, moccasins, a blackened cross, oiled deer-skin leggings, and the blanket wrapped around the trapper. Then, not far from the pack, she found the thief of health: the soup of deer brains with which the man had be-gun to cure a hide.

Still holding Elisabeth, Cath made a bird's nest of dry shredded grass and some of last year's thistledown she had gathered weeks earlier. Blowing on coals poured from her clay pot, she added dry twigs, then kindling and logs from the trapper's woodpile. After the fire had begun to leap and play with vigor, she shoved the birchbark container with its gray mixture into the fire's heart, afraid of poisoning the water if she emptied the bowl in the stream, afraid Elisabeth might find the mess if she threw it into the woods. Perhaps he had cut himself when scraping hair from the deerskin; perhaps he had thought little of such a nick. Cath hated to part with the half-prepared hide, but she dragged it outside the camp, anchoring the center with stones. If he woke, the trapper might want the deerskin that had cost him so much.

During the afternoon and evening Cath dripped water into the man's mouth. The tongue looked slightly swollen, pinched and white around the edges. She bathed his forehead and torso, hoping to cool his fever. Elisabeth plunged to sleep before dark, worn out by the strange day of watching. When Cath woke the next morning the baby was already squatting at the man's head, rubbing the blanket up and down on his face.

"Eye peep," Elisabeth said. "Peep eye peep."

Cath snatched at the blanket, turning it

back from the face, and pulled her daughter away. "Hush, Elisabeth. Hush, my sweet." Since the last time she had given him water in the night something had changed. His eyes were open but unseeing, and a faint red net mottled his skin. For an hour she sat moistening his mouth with water while Elisabeth ate blueberries picked the day before, smearing purple on her face and hands. "Good buwies," she said. "Mo." Afterward Cath washed the baby and foraged in the woods, returning soon to sit by the trapper. She felt weary, leaden, although now and then she longed to shake him, shout out her questions, demand to know where were others—where were the posts, trappers, forts, settlements, Indian villages? Where was she? Which way should she go? About midday the trapper's eyes focused on mother and child. Elisabeth stood in Cath's lap, hands on her mother's shoulders, curls bright with sun.

"Ah. Fah," he said with an effort, closing his eyes.

Cath dribbled water on his lips, but he did not open his eyes again. Since he might be able to hear, she asked him where they were and which way to go next. Repeating her questions over and over, she spoke slowly and close to his ear, though she felt almost certain that the trapper was no Englishman. When he did not respond, she sat back, watching him for any change, wiping her eyes.

"No use to moan," she whispered.

She began to recite a few prayers, then a portion of the litany. An hour later she still bathed his forehead, but she no longer believed he would survive, no longer even expected him to swim up to consciousness. If only she had arrived earlier. If only he could have told her where they were—if only he carried a map marked with an X, with a post, with a settlement. On the clearing's edge, hope had flown to her hand, quivering and palpable as a bird seeking refuge from the sea. But it seemed she was only a small ratchet down the wheel in the trapper's fortune, that he made no difference in her own, no difference to her daughter. Naked in the warm afternoon sun, Elisabeth hunkered down on her haunches and stared, the tip of her forefinger making circles in the dirt.

The red net under the trapper's skin grew more distinct. Death was fishing with his purse seine, Cath thought, and soon would be dragging bottom with the trapper's heavy weight. She left his side for a few minutes to pick some mint and to rescue supper from her hastily built fish trap. When she returned Elisabeth was squatting by the fire, ululating softly. Cath hoped she had lost interest in the trapper. After gutting a trout and spitting it for the fire, Cath splashed water on the child's dirty buttocks and legs, hurriedly dressing her for night.

At sunset the trapper still lived, but his breath moved more slowly than before, making a clogged noise. Elisabeth, full of fish and berries, stamped in a wild circuit of the fire. She danced flat-footed, stomping a halo around the trapper's head, laughing and backing away when Cath snatched at her gown.

"You be awake," Cath said, startled. The trapper's eyes were open, fixed on the dancing figure. His tongue worked in his mouth, but he could not speak. Elisabeth dragged her gown off again, rumpling her curls and revealing her shape, still a baby's large-headed and potbellied form, every curve and tuck of skin, every tangle of hair needful and right: perfection. In the firelight she was a Midas child, a daughter more rare and valuable than any coin. Stumbling, she pitched into her mother's lap.

"Ma. Fall down. Ma. See dan," she called, clutching her mother's bodice. "I see thee," Cath said, stroking her naked back. "Higgledy piggledy, my sweet babe," she sang. The trapper still stared as Cath pulled the nightgown back over the baby's head.

Kneeling by the man's side, Cath saw it was too late for speech or help. A white froth crawled from one corner of the trapper's mouth. The wet burdensome noise stopped, leaving a space for the snap of sparks, the child's small breath, the evening breeze skating over the lake and blowing the rag of a soul away beyond the trees, beyond stars. *To the throne of God*, Cath thought, still kneeling, with Elisabeth tugging at her arm.

The floor of heaven was littered with stars. Now Selene the moon peeped at a bloated dead man and a sleeping child, curled in her mother's lap, at a mother sitting very straight with firelight reflected in her unblinking eyes. And though the moon shone on town and country alike, and though it seemed she could have told them where the tiny English settlements were flung down in the wilderness, she was stone-dead and cold and could not speak.

The Pillicock Hills

The trapper's face, the color of gray mud, lingered in Cath's mind. *Like a bloody-bones, a bull-beggar.* She could not bury him, though she prayed for his soul, whispering into the fire. Walking north, she kept remembering how they left his body to rot, dressed in the hunting shirt which she slit down the sides and sleeves in order to get it on his unyielding body. *Decay. Grains of dust locked in the cabinet of God.* She took with her the skillet, the hatchet and knife, moccasins, blanket, string, and the splint pack with its leather straps, comfortable to wear on her back. The blanket stank of musk and animals and, even after soaking and airing, smelled wild.

For three days she continued along the shore until she reached the lake's outlet. She traveled short distances, intent on keeping the blanket and heavy tools. Following a creek that flowed from the lake, she came to a river, and though finding it not so large as the Hudson below Albany, she hoped it might prove to be the same river. She and Elisabeth pushed north up the valley until the river shrank, no more than a large creek. Fish being plentiful in the streams, and berries beginning to ripen on warm slopes and burned-over fields, Cath felt secure in following the water north, foraging in streams and foothills. She camped by the thin teardrop of water, and two days later tracked around a second pond. She found no large lake crowned by an English fort and felt that the creek leading her north could not be the same broad river that eased past Albany, streaming to the sea. Now she understood that to the north stood mountains and, it seemed, many minor lakes and few of the promised trappers. The world was so empty! She saw that leaving the Indian women had been a mistake, and that abandoning any human help from now on would be the gravest of errors. To the west lay wilderness with no hope of rescue. To the south, she assumed, the unfordable river tumbled from west to east; somewhere below that water, creeks and rivulets must flow into the Hudson. But she was unsure. Where was the east-running river? Fording the water in stony shallows, she journeyed south, moving along the eastern bank of the creek. Soon it swelled into a river. A third, she thought, perhaps pouring into the east-running river. The map she imagined was mutable as water; arguing with herself, pushing south, she at last made up her mind to travel eastward. If she could only keep to the east, she might find a settlement or Mahican camp, and failing that, eventually gain the coast where lay seaports and fishing villages.

Fear at her throat; having passed through several gaps between hills, Cath found herself in a corridor between hills to the west and mountains to the east. She began drifting south under the green shadow of mountains, seeking a wide inlet. She had come so far to be locked in by the landscape! It was a cold century, a cold summer, and the gloom of mountains chilled Cath. She feared having made an error, perhaps merely the last in a series of mistakes, despite all her thought and prayers.

Always she feared the coming of winter, feared she would wander into a desert region barren of food; several mornings she had spotted hundreds of turkeys crossing the valley but could not catch one. Cath had lost count of the days but guessed the date must be mid-August or later. Elisabeth fed well on late summer's berries—raspberries, dewberries, blackberries, huckleberries—but almost none of the dried meat remained. At least the pack was lighter to carry. Cath picked black chokecherries and snapped off the delicate heads of elderberry bushes, saving them to strip clean by the fire. Every afternoon she spread blueberries in the sun, raking them across a smock to dry beside the fire. She and Elisabeth ate mice and insects, mostly ants, though Catherwood rolled larvae and bugs in sorrel or violet leaves, biting down quickly and swallowing hard.

For two weeks she traveled south, passing a lake, later following the guide of a creek. When it forked, she kept to the east branch, passing south of mountains, north of further ranges of hills. Elisabeth played along the stream, picking up leaves and pebbles. Twice she and Cath had fevers, but the baby recovered quickly. Several times she suffered from diarrhea, and Cath dosed her with a tea made from silverweed, collected weeks before. In a day or two Elisabeth would be laughing, jumping on her mother with excitement. They played a game while Cath foraged, calling back and forth *aa, aa* in cries that made Elisabeth laugh with abandon, eyes shut and mouth wide open. Cath kept her in close range, using the call whenever her daughter—squatting on her haunches to eat ants and low berries—seemed to disappear.

For months past, Elisabeth had spent most of her time curled in Cath's lap, riding on her shoulders, or asleep in her arms. It seemed natural to both of them that this should be so. The little girl would back up without needing to look and brush against Cath, dropping down with a thump in her lap. Worming a way under the blanket, she pressed close to her mother, matching her shape for shape. Everything that was sentimental in their bond had been pared away by the wilderness, until both mother and child knew the great longing and need for each other as their strong tie to life. Outside somewhere lay Gabriel, Lacey, Jamie, and the others. The link to Gabriel held firm, vivid and alive whenever Cath allowed herself to think of home. And beyond the stars, beyond time and space, like a brightening behind a door, sparkled the souls of her adopted mother, Fanny, even the nameless trapper. Nevertheless, hour by hour, what remained important to Cath was the round of cleaning and feeding her child, caring for her in sickness or play, warming her with food and fire. And just as Catherwood herself became a shelter and secure space for Elisabeth, so Elisabeth gave her the courage to thrust forward through the vast spaces of wilderness without trembling, simply gathering the child a little closer as she stepped into the wide prospect of a valley or looked up at a waving line of hills.

The land they reached between the mountains was sloped and green, with eagles in the high clouds, with big panels of light that swept gleaming across the scrub of burned-over meadows and dense forests.

Where the creek petered out among hills, Cath came upon the remains of an Indian camp, the ashes smeared on the ground by past rains. Digging in a cache already raided by animals, she found only spoiled pumpkin and a mud-sealed pot of corn and beans, which she broke open; they spent the night in the abandoned camp, where Cath built new fire on the grave of the old.

It seemed September, when the drenched green hills shone in waning light. "These be magic. These be the Pillicock hills," Cath said, touching her daughter's nose with a fingertip. She and Elisabeth sought passages between low mountains, camping when they could on borderland between hill and valley, between forest and meadow. Humped in the distance, small animals packed in their end-of-summer wares. Bears feasted on slopes of blueberries, their claws jeweled with fruit. Autumn began to conquer the fields, mingling late summer's eupatorium with troops of blue and purple asters and goldenrod, spattering the blueberry leaves with fire. Picking a twig of blue-black juniper berries, Cath breathed in the spicy fragrance. She foraged in bogs, gathering cranberries barely linked to their trailing branches by hairspring stems. "Bird meat," Elisabeth said, spitting in distaste. There were acorns and hickory nuts, boletes and pitted morels, chanterelles smelling of apricots, wild grapes. Cath, always hungry, feared she might be passing by good food, feared to eat much of what she saw. "Still, my Elisabeth," she said, "there be manna enough to live in the wilderness."

A pin-fine rain sieved slantwise from gauzy clouds almost every afternoon. One day the temperature cooled and a sparse snow flew through the air, some aerial sleight of hand seeming to juggle the stars so that not one landed on earth. Although unsure when the date would come, she guessed she had until Hallowmas to find a village; after that she could not be certain of the weather or of finding food in the woods. Elisabeth refused so much food, often spitting out even cooked fruit as too sour, too sharp in taste. "No likey, no likey," she shouted, indignant and hungry. Surely, Cath thought, they would find a settlement before November, even at this slow pace, even trudging on with her ripped boots tucked inside the trapper's big moccasins.

Sunny days came on with nights unexpectedly cool. On their seventh day in the hills Elisabeth woke with a fever, and Cath spent the day collecting brush and wood for the fire, gathering food with the child held in her arms. When ill, she seemed to draw her arms and legs inward, becoming younger and more helpless. Catherwood cleaned her face with leaves, washing her body once with water heated in the skillet. The little girl clung to her, wrapping both arms around her neck.

"Chin," she said, "fingahs, my ma." Elisabeth gently explored her mother's face, poking a finger in her mouth, drawing a line along her jaw.

"How I love thee," Catherwood said, rubbing her cool cheek against Elisabeth's hot face. Like a font at the bottom of the sea, she thought, streaming from forever and forever to fill the world up with ocean and buoy great ships stacked with sail. And to toss up mermaids and curious monsters from the deep.

"So much I love thee, under Pillicock hills," Cath said.

The day hurtled into dark and cold, and when Cath woke the next morning an easterly black frost sleeved the firs at the edge of the woods, and here and there a spear of cold had made shrubs and leafy stalks into tattered banners. Fear surged, a frost at her throat. Elisabeth lay limp and hot against her breast, and when Cath lifted the blanket and cloak from her arms, she saw that the child's arms trembled. Cradling Elisabeth in one arm, she added wood to the fire, heating a tea of dried red clover heads and mint leaves. The little girl nursed, eagerly at first, then turning away to press her red cheek against the breast. All morning Cath swabbed her face and arms with cool water, but there was little change. The stern ache at her throat grew. Cath could hardly bend her thoughts to pray. She shivered, remembering the dying trapper and how he stared intently at the child. *Dear God*, she prayed, *dear God, let this not, dear God.*

"Da," Elisabeth said, her eyes closed. "Mama."

"Minimy pinimy, where is she? Minimy pinimy, I do see," Cath whispered, but her daughter was quiet and still.

All day Cath held her beside the fire, moistening her lips with tea. Red-faced and burning, Elisabeth would eat nothing, not even the sweetest dried berries. Once she vomited a little acorn mast, but afterward seemed unchanged.

In the evening Cath laid on enough wood for a bonfire, moving their woven shelter closer to its warmth. She sat cross-legged by the flames and held the waking child in her arms, rested the sleeping child in her lap. The fever did not break, and twice the little girl shook violently. At dawn Cath cleaned her with tepid water and was alarmed by the red and white blotches on her belly and back. Elisabeth's breath made a bubbling sound, and she did not stir for most of the morning. In late afternoon she drank a few sips of tea, lying listlessly against her mother. Still hot, she had stopped urinating some time in the morning.

"My Elisabeth," Cath said, "my sweet-heart."

Tears flooded her eyes, blurred the child's face, hanging and plummeting in big pendant drops.

"Try, my little maid," she said, moistening the baby's lips.

Elisabeth made a faint sound of kissing, heartening her mother.

"My sweet. Stay," Cath said, lowering her face close to the child's face.

For a long time Elisabeth gazed into her mother's eyes, loosely grasping Cath's fore-finger. Then she slept. Cath ate a few berries, watching her daughter's face, listening to the watery sound of her breath. Close to sunset, the baby woke again, and she and Cath looked at each other while the sun's spent coin sank lower and lower, its final beams cresting the Pillicock hills.

"Cock crowed on Pillicock hill," Cath said, repeating a phrase from a rhyme the child loved.

Elisabeth reached up her hand, the fingers curled, and Cath bent to kiss her on the lips.

"My sweetest babe," she whispered.

Around and about, the little animals sought tunnels and bolt holes against the night, diving into the Pillicock hills, and the leaf-and-berry-crowned bears slumbered. There was nothing left of England or York, nor of Virginia or Massachusetts; there was only the mother holding the child upon her lap, one small hand partially raised, the fingers curled. There was nothing but the pin-pricked stars and the moon, a coin of base metal. The sound of rabbits and wood-chucks snuffling into place in warm burrows, the deep breathing of bears, the breathing of the mother: the small absence, the child crumpled and cooling in the mother's arms.

"Suffer," Cath whispered. She had meant to say, *Suffer the little children,* but could not.

The Child
and the Four Elements

Catherwood rocked the dead child on her lap, weeping as she repeated the burial service. All morning she said the words, over and over, leaning across the baby as the fire sank onto its bed of coals. There was no one to make her give up the body, no one to offer prayers and anthems but herself. By afternoon she was ill and prayed that she might die and join the child who had never been away from her side. *For Elisabeth will be afeared without me, for she is small and the throne room of heaven so large.* She fell asleep with the body in her arms and woke an hour later, instantly remembering Elisabeth, crying out loudly as though the loss had happened only a moment before. That night she built a huge fire, fearing animals, and slept with her hand on the baby's stomach.

In the morning Cath felt starved, and she carried the baby with her as she picked berries on a sunny slope. She moved slowly up the hill, raking the bushes with one hand. Morning prayers jostled in her head but gave no comfort. Between mouthfuls she cried out and shouted her grief, letting the tears drench her face without wiping them away. She breakfasted as she had seen bears eat, shoving fruit peppered with leaves and stems in her open noisy mouth.

Later she washed the baby in cold water, handling her gently. Death had gleaned all sign of translucent and rosy life from her skin, and like a child's much-handled cloth baby, she was gray, here and there marred further by the remains of old rashes and mosquito bites. Cath wet and picked the tangles from the knotted hair, remembering how Henry had caressed the back of Elisabeth's head, saying it was as curly as a lamb's bottom. So much curlier, so much longer now. The arms of Christ, Cath thought, must be weary and aching with the weight of the world's lambs. Surely God pitied her when the cold night air stole the health from her only child.

She could not bear to bury her daughter, could not think of leaving her in cold ground. The end of fall would come on strong, days of long red leaf fall, days of dropping yellow. Frost would latch on the bare ground, send down tap roots of ice to where Elisabeth slept like a seed. Then king winter, prowling the forest, shedding snow. Everywhere would glitter with scepters of ice, ice flow massed until a dim green glimmered in the inmost chamber of unearthly castles. Where a child could never live.

Then, too, would come a further loss. Now she could touch her child, wash her body and arrange the hair. How many steps would it take for her to lose what remained of Elisabeth? After so many months of care, to just slip away between trees . . . "I cannot," Cath said. "Cannot." She imagined that for a few minutes she would look back and know where the grave lay. Then for a mile, perhaps, if she was watchful, she would know enough to retrace her steps. But there would come a moment where the forest seemed to shake itself free of even that one ordering point. Then she would swing free of all knowledge of place, helplessly weaving on and on.

When dark drew across the camp, Catherwood lay for another night between fire and Elisabeth. She slept in snatches, toward dawn dreaming that Elisabeth, a newborn baby, sailed like Moses in a woven boat. The basket hung up on cobbles, swirled and dipped in fast water. Once a wave slapped and swamped the boat, and the baby sank to the bottom, her hands out. Red efts wriggled next to her open eyes. Cath waded in the stream, hurting her feet on stones as she rushed to right the boat, placing the baby back inside. Slipping into the water behind her daughter, Cath let the stream drag her over sand and shillets. The dream made her fluent as a mermaid, spun her past rocks, shot her under waterfalls while the boat bobbed east on widening rivers, twirling cork-like toward the roar of the sea. She speared through shoals of darting silver and green and crested on the Atlantic rollers, tumbled under and over the green slapdash waves of ocean. A mile out she floated, face down in the water, staring as the basket gyred downward in a cloud of bubbles. Sinking deeper, she caught sight of a sail.

"Bird. John Bird," she cried.

Cath woke, her face wet from tears and dew.

She could not bury the child in water, but she did make a basket from canes and vines. Since Elisabeth had drawn her legs up before she died, the radden-basket and its lid were oval. It was afternoon before Cath finished, although she worked quickly with her rough materials. Then she coiled dry grasses into a nest, draping Elisabeth's cloak on top. After cutting away some curls with Gabriel's knife, she placed the child's wooden doll under her raised hand. Teeth marks grooved the flat face, scoring the bun of hair. Elisabeth was dressed in her nightgown, stained with fruit but fine with tucks and a minute parade of buttons and buttonholes that had cost Cath many hours of care.

Remembering a tale of Indian burials, she climbed into the low branches of a tree, lashing the basket to a crotch with vines. She left it there for two hours, but when dark fell, she tore the vines away and carried the basket back to her shelter.

The next morning she began to dig, chopping the soil with the trapper's iron-headed hatchet. She tried cutting the earth with a knife, sawing wedges of dirt, prying them out of the ground with the flat cheek of the blade. Stones, stakes: nothing worked well. She clawed the ground with her bare hands, ripping a nail to the quick so that she wept, thinking about how she had carefully nipped and peeled away the tips of Elisabeth's nails, leaving a sprinkled trail of new moons, invisible in the forest. By midafternoon Cath had torn a raw pit in the ground, deep enough for a child's burial. Somewhere close by, she heard the ragged noise of her own breath, her own voice. There seemed a self to dig and sweat, another to gasp and cry. Before dark she placed the basket in the pit and closed the hole.

Filthy, hungry, Cath hurried to collect wood. She stripped off her clothes in the cold, scrubbing herself in an achingly cold stream before huddling by the fire in cloak and blanket. Sleep, a dark place without dreams, jerked her from the day.

In the morning she arranged the trapper's

pack, then foraged for food in the stream and on a sunny hillside. She climbed to the hilltop, determining where her path lay, then walked a few hundred yards farther on. Her arms felt strangely light, as if they might lift and fly up to her shoulders, face, toward the sky. Afterward she returned to the camp, setting down the pack.

"Christ have mercy on me," she said. "Christ have mercy."

She began to scoop the dirt in fistfuls from the grave, at first steadily, but soon with more and more energy, as if she thought to rescue her daughter from the black ground, from being buried alive. Hurling the earth away, she tore at the ground, crying out when stones cut her hands, when a nail split. The weight at her throat, the weight of soil on her daughter's limbs: she could not endure that heaviness an instant longer. Short, panting groans pushed from her throat. She must thrust the baby from the maw of grave, must raise earth from her face. The minutes sweated, earth sluggish on its axis. At last the egg, smeared with mud but whole, was pulled with a sucking sound from the pit.

Another dawn and Cath began again,

heaping branches on the fire. Elisabeth lay on a bed of hurdles, her hand still lifted slightly over the carved doll. All day the child burned in the fire, and each time when Cath added wood, she swaddled cloth around her head, afraid she might smell the roasting flesh. She knelt by a second, smaller fire, weary, wordless, her ears ringing. Next morning she raked the ashes with her hands, fishing the large and small bones from the dust. Patiently she combed the site until she was sure every bone that could live through fire lay on Elisabeth's cloak. She rolled the bones in one of the child's smocks, knotting each end with the trapper's string. Then she folded the cloak around the smock and used the last of the string to secure the package, knobbled and irregular. Still, the bundle of bones and broken skull was surprisingly light and small.

"Christ forgive me," Catherwood said, kneeling a long time in the ashes, the knotted shape in her lap.

The death was ended, save for coming days without comfort, with cold. Whatever happened, the bones of mother and child would not be divided.

* * *

Catherwood moved south and east for the next weeks, carrying the bones, allowing the terrain and river to guide her path. It seemed she had shed all fear when Elisabeth died. No expanse of valley, no height of hill could frighten; these were but little rooms next to eternity. And while she had once feared sitting in the same room with a dead body, now the child shadowed her everywhere, a presence, a sorrow that matched her steps. After the first week she found, with slight surprise, that she no longer wished to die, and yet death was not fearsome. *For I can bear to be like my child.*

No fire could be too warm in these days. Cath dreamed of crawling into the heart of flames with Elisabeth in her arms, dreamed of a flower unfurling its petals of fire. Cold clenched the hills, even in the brightest sun.

The forest hummed around her, each noise blurred into a background for grief. There were no childish plosives, no constant stream leafed with words. How much company Elisabeth had been, her fairy laughter rippling the fabric of the wilderness. She had tasted sound, puffed air out, pushed it from the back of her throat, growled and worried syllables, sung them in single bird notes—

like a fairy tale in which a family of stepsisters speaks newts and toads, speaks gold coins and roses. Each dawn when she swam up from sleep, Catherwood could almost hear Elisabeth's small murmur. *When I die, dear God, let me hear that voice.*

Food became more difficult to harvest, and she grew weak from diarrhea after having scavenged frozen songbirds and rotten deer meat. She raked up roots of arrowhead and spatterdock, but this was no place of pools and streams. Fifteen days after Elisabeth's death, Cath found three young apple trees seeded by birds. Cranberry vines still produced fruit, and she boiled acorns mixed with fruit in the skillet. On days when she found little or no food, she chewed on wintergreen berries and leaves, calming her hunger with their spicy flavor. A hard frost blackened more plants, leaving her with even less to eat. She rationed herself to a handful of dried fruit a day, together with whatever acorns and roots or insects she could find. With the increasing cold came a dreamy lethargy, and there were mornings when she longed only to sleep. Even the clang and flurry of immense flocks of geese and ducks or the whinnying chortle of a loon could not hold her attention. The baby at her back, she pushed southeast along the river, forcing herself to walk each day until the sun passed noon. A soft sun poured around her steps, a honeyed light that seemed to drench her veins with sleep. *A wilderness of effort*, she whispered, counting her steps. She counted them over and over from one to one thousand, one to one thousand. Steps to a dream.

Earlier faces came back to her in these days, faces of Lacey, Jamie, her mother Elisabeth, Gaffer Withycombe among his roses. She dreamed of telling stories by the fire at home; she dreamed that her mother rocked Elisabeth, singing in the chimney corner. Ceaselessly she dreamed, scarcely remembering to eat from her slender hoard of fruit and nuts. Only Gabriel never found a place in her dreams, and now the thread that ran between them lay loose in Cath's hand. An hour or a day more and she might let the floss drift like a spider's floating line. Then evergreen shadows would cover up its white ravel, final leaves would flutter down on Catherwood, and she and Elisabeth would stay forever in the forest.

She remembered a story her mother had

told, a story from her childhood, when she lived in a stone house east of Mother Childe, the herb woman they sometimes visited for remedies. The family and some servants in the house suddenly became ill with fevers and agues, with sweating and painful throats, all of them so weak they could not stand or walk. The servants who remained sound ran away, leaving the family and three servants helpless. Most were in the bedchambers, but Elisabeth and another child lay too weak to move on a soiled bed in the parlor. Sun filled up the room, and Elisabeth and her brother Edmund floated feverishly in the light. One morning her father, the last to be taken ill, dragged himself to their room. His head rested against the bedstead, and his arms were frail and insubstantial. Elisabeth grazed his forehead with the palm of her hand. After a few hours he crawled away again, leaving the children a bottle of beer and a bottle of dill water. Then for many days they lay alone, neither of them speaking or touching, each empty of everything but the great white light in the day and the autumn cold and darkness at night, each dreaming clearly and calmly with childish stoic fatalism that the other had died, each silent with parched mouth, burning with fever, curled motionless in filth. The light went on and on, like an endless desert.

Tap, tap, tap: the sound came from another world, calling them to fly up—they must have flown because they could no longer walk—and over to the window. There stood Mother Childe summoning them back to earth, wrapped in her burred cloak, grasping a long pole, and hooked to one end a basket containing a chicken simmered in herbs, jellies, and bottles of curious liquids. The children ate the food and grew stronger, sucking on the stripped bones, licking the wooden trencher.

But there was no Mother Childe for Catherwood, not one in all the forests of America, though week by week she grew lighter. Already she knew what her mother's story had meant, knew moments when she floated on the autumn light.

Adrift, only lightly tethered to a body sinking by degrees, she came upon the burnt stumps of three houses. Cath wandered fitfully through the landscape of stobs and gleaned a little corn where volunteer stalks lay at full length in a scrubby field. Like a ghost she paced between the broken foundations, restless, unwilling to leave the scorched timber. A brick oven hunched alone in a field, sheltering bread and pies hardened to stone. That night she slept rolled in the trapper's blanket beside a fire, too tired to make a shelter. On the following morning she found seven marked trees, and then for many minutes she stood staring at smoke wavering to the southeast. *Never so weary. Never. If only there were no smoke.* She was ready to burrow and sleep, to wait for the cold to close down.

1678

The Raven's House

Awkward and alarming, the rote noise flayed the edges of the woods. Catherwood followed the sound past evergreens and leaf litter and into the sunlight of bare enclosed fields. *Cow clats. Arrish. A dead barrow-pig, hooves in air*. She hid her basket under a chestnut snapped in two by lightning, and while it occurred to her to change the trapper's moccasins for the silk stockings and sea-green slippers she had carried such a long way, she did not. She took from the pack only the package of bones and the box for flints that now held Elisabeth's curls. She forced box and package through a rent in the lining of her cloak. Nothing stirred in the bleak light which spread evenly over broken stalks, an abandoned harrow studded with iron spikes, a two-wheeled cart loaded with cakes of manure. She walked on, passing palisades in need of repair, a dugout, mud-and-wattle huts, and unpainted boxes with steep roofs and tacked-on additions. They clustered hard on a dirt road, facing south, showing her their muddy backsides. Cath had not eaten since the day before and hesitated, dizzy, remembering the few dried berries left in her pack. Sun swam on her face, brightening light that made her reel. Then the noise swelled, a clash of voices without common pitch or tempo. She paused, unable to think for the sun that kept getting in her eyes. The light, noise, the dogs come from nowhere—was this a home of living people? Barking and springing in the air, the town dogs pursued her, baring their teeth. Catherwood breathed heavily, pitching and staggering toward the disorderly noise. Her eyes were wide open as she neared a square building, fortified with close-dug stakes and pocked with bounty heads of wolves. She closed her eyes against the weatherbeaten snouts of wolves, the snarling muzzles of curs; and when she opened them again, a man was rushing toward her, brandishing a stave. From the south side of the church streamed children and groups of men and women dressed in russet and Lincoln green and fillemot. Bewildered, she stared at a man dressed in rags and smeared with dirt and ashes, a word pasted to his forehead. The wind blew the figures to her, so many dead leaves hurtled in a glittering light. The high twanging of voices struck at the light, reaching her as if from a distance, so that she called back to them, protesting. Then a great black raven in a skullcap and cape flew to her side, gripping her arm. Her eyes dazzled; black flecks like a hundred tiny kites lazed through the light, joined by a thousand and then another thousand until the beating of their wings shut out the thrumming voices and their uplifted capes and black skullcapped heads blotted out the sun.

Cath let go, sinking down to a dark shire of sleep, an undersea place where even John Bird's sail could not find her. From time to time she surfaced, choking on the tinctures spooned into her mouth. Once she woke to find the raven perched in her room, his side-long eye resting on her face. She met his gaze and he smiled in surprise, but then Cath heard a baby's cry and dived back down into darkness.

Later she waked to find herself alone, the room under the eaves empty save for the bed, a crude chair with her own cloak hanging from one finial, and a drawing of a child tacked to the plaster wall. Sun whirled through the quarrels in prismatic quirks and curls. The builders must have pieced the window from new clear glass and older, salvaged quarrels gone amethyst. It was a poor room, but a fire of mixed green and dry wood sparkled on the hearth. Cath crawled out of bed, splashed her face with water from a bowl she found on the floor, then reached for her cloak in quick alarm—seeing it brushed clean of ash and mud. She draped the cloak over her shoulders, reaching in the lining to touch the box and the package of bones. *Elisabeth, safe.* She felt filthy; her hair a dank and heavy coil, her thighs and arms moist.

"I be not dead, this is no heaven or hell," she said, trembling, resting her forehead on the thick, cold quarrels.

On the sill a wasp no bigger than a thumb-nail warmed itself in the sunlight, chafing shanks and hips, combing its velvet. Motion-less, Catherwood watched the busy, twid-dling movements.

"Spark clasped in apple-drane so small," she whispered.

"She is nimble, neat in her jacket and hel-met," the raven said at her back. He craned forward, looking quickly at her face, her eyes. "Do I startle you, madam?"

"Months ago," Cath said, "all surprise died in me."

"Madam, good day," he said. "I hope you fare better than we have yet seen."

He wore a close-fitting velvet cap against the cold, with flaps that covered his ears. His beak, pinched with cold; his eyes bright, questioning. The mouth ran straight across. When the voice echoed in the room, Cath strained to catch its unfamiliar accent. *Harsh, like a raven's croak and caw.*

"You be a man, then," Cath said, slipping to the floor.

"Madam, you are not yourself." Raven or man, he helped her to the chair. "And yet who are you, may I ask? What is your name, your place? Who are your people? For that you are none of us I see."

"My mother loved to greet travelers. And any not like us," Cath said, slumping over to rest her head on the coverlet.

"Your name?"

"Catherwood," she whispered, her eye rambling down a white stitched line.

"Your name," she repeated.

"Mr. Taylor, of Westfield. Minister of this place, physician to you and its citizens, public man, farmer, would-be scholar."

Tealor, tealor, tealor rang in Cath's ears. Near her eye was a clawed place in the coverlet, crazily mended once in dun cotton thread, once in green silk. *Ripped by talons.*

"Thread," she said loudly. "No tailor."

"You are ill, Mistress Catherwood."

A little unraveled tendril of red silk thread poked in the air.

"What country is this, Mr. Taylor?"

"Truly I believe your presence here to be remarkable and strange," he said. "We are people of Westfield, on the river branch known by the same name, in the Connecticut valley and in the colony of Massachusetts in New England."

Dissenters. "Ravens," Cath said, and fell

asleep, one cheek pressed against the green silk stitches.

In the afternoon she drank some mutton broth and a stinking herbal tea but vomited shortly after. She lay propped on bolsters, feeling sweaty and hollow. *Brickle as glass. As eggs in a frail.* The cloak hung again from the finial, belling outward on the floor. She could hear the baby again, hopeless in its grief. A woman Mr. Taylor introduced to her as Goodwife Dumbleton came to empty the basin of vomit, nodding to her.

"A baby," whispered Catherwood.

"Mrs. Taylor was brought to bed t'other week, madam," the woman said. "James is a grouty babe enough.

"Her last child, Elizabeth, died last year," she added.

Cath turned her face to the wall. Amethyst trickled over the plaster, shadowing the child's chalk portrait. *Grief is the shade of amethyst stone.* The purple quarrels darkened, and shadows pooled in the corners of the room. Tears soaked Cath's hair, rose and balanced on her lashes, plunged down her cheekbones. The raven looked at her in the dark, swiveling his luminous eye. His silver cup tasted of oil and peppermint and something else.

White oak bark.

Had she spoken?

"You may be a better physicker than I, Mistress Catherwood."

Mistress Catherwood. What a funny name the raven chose for her. Sleep like a glossy wing stretched over her head. *Beam feathers.* "Ravenous," she muttered. "Sleep."

When she waked again, light spangled the ceiling. A three-year-old child in breeches and a deer-colored waistcoat taped in red stood studying her from the middle of the room. She gazed back at him, her mind clear and level for the first time in many days. He looked like an English boy, his shoulder-length yellow hair cut straight above his brows, his eyes an unwavering blue, his cheeks rosy.

"Sam, Sam, come here," a voice called from downstairs.

Sam did not move until his scrutiny was complete.

"I not sick, I happy," he announced.

A stray smile touched Cath's lips, and the boy charged from the room. "Not dead," she said aloud. "By the will of God, I be not dead." This very day she would write to Gabriel's agent in Albany. Surely the raven would know an enterprising man with a compass and horse in Westfield, however far from Albany, willing to carry a letter now that the harvest was ended. Not a raven. Not a bird but a man. *Tealor.* Mr. Taylor would choose the messenger, for no dissenter would want her to linger long, tainting his household and town with Church of England ways. Gabriel would pay the traveler well in gold, or in whatever coin he desired. Gabriel would make it worth any man's while.

Bescummered. Beastled.

"Pray, bathe, eat," she said aloud. *Get on with living.* Had she ever been so dank and filthy? After all, it seemed she cared, it seemed she lived again.

Cath peered out a chink in the window, examining the square meetinghouse hemmed with palisades, the muddy houses, a brindled cow scraping her backside against a rocking fence. *A barton. Straw bee-butts. Rotting bean haulm. A donnick.* Quivering with effort, she plugged the hole again with a twist of kersey and tottered back to the bed. At the beginning of the week Sarah

Dumbleton had aired the bedding and boiled the tow linens, which had clung, frozen and stiff, to the back fence. They were rough against the skin but at least they no longer stank. Cath dragged the cloak onto her body, shaking from the cold and a low fever. Flicking weakly on its bed of embers, the fire gave little heat, and only a spindly November light illuminated the room.

The house swarmed with noise. Jamie shrieked, his mother's voice a weary monotone counterpoint to his cries. Somewhere Sam was singing, and a distant thudding came from the hall, where Goodwife Dumbleton was making bread.

Cath picked out Mr. Taylor's voice from the buzzing. Now and then she heard him, testing out lines for a sermon before he copied them down. Whether drawn by a passion for words or by his interest in healing, Mr. Taylor had recorded the phrases Catherwood spoke in delirium. Later he gave her a scrap of paper, covered on both sides: *Gold washt face. More light. Elizabeth. Sweete babe. Bird under sea. Body. Wicker cage. Sail to sea. Elizabeth. Elizabeth. Elizabeth. Gabriel. Gold on ground. Elizabeth on fire.*

She burned the paper, watching it twist and flame out.

Cath felt there was no niche for her in the house, not only because the four rooms were crabbed and uncomfortable, frequently busy with visitors and petitioners, but because she was no dissenter. Perhaps that was what made her chamber under the eaves seem airless and tight. Gabriel seemed impossibly far away, farther than when she had pushed through unmarked forest, despite the Westfield man who had left on a borrowed horse, riding toward Albany. He would meet with their agent, then ride on to Gabriel. She shivered under the cloak, pressing her hands over her ears to keep out all sound. Only then could she imagine Elisabeth, the smell of her, the silky skin, tangled tendrils of curls.

There might be space for a lost woman in his four rooms, a refuge within earth's four corners, but there would be no chamber in the raven's heaven for Elisabeth. Cath could not let herself hear the lines, the sermons that wound upward like household smoke. If the words crept to her door they would darken more than a room, and she would be left with nothing but bones.

A Rainbow for Crows

"You are not hearty, madam, you are not strong," Mr. Taylor said; "you are something better but subject to these feverish fits."

He explained to Cath that when she grew well, Tithingman Cornish would come to question her, as he did each stranger in the twelve families he oversaw. "For we receive only such as may be of one heart with us." But she was not able, he repeated, not fit for questioning. "I bade him wait. The selectman and people would not meet to judge this case until, madam, you are yourself again."

"Myself again."

"Yes."

Cath sat on a bench by the hall fire, patching a smock with a square of old cotton. Even so near to the fire, the dirt floor chilled her feet, now clad in the slippers from her pack.

For an instant fear gleamed as she remembered stories of Massachusetts Bay, mobs of townspeople scourging women or chasing them into forests feathered with arrows. Then fear fluttered away again. What could they do to her that had not been done already? And she was of no outlaw religion.

"I be not afraid of man judgment," she said softly. "I be not afraid of any man or woman, Indian or dissenter, Quaker or Roman."

"Papist elves," Mr. Taylor muttered.

The bone needle dipped over and under, over and under, then tugged its puckered wake behind.

Earlier Cath had stitched up the rents in the yellow silk lining to her cloak and mended a hole in the wool. No one could draw the bones and hair from their hiding place without ripping the fabric open. She still wore her gown and silk petticoat, most of the tatters hidden under patches of Kendal green. "I be a fine motley clown," she said aloud. At first when she had ventured to walk on the commons and water meadows, Cath had folded her cloak close around her body, hiding her vivid colors, although even the rose-colored cloak was as startling as an out-of-season flower on a forest floor of winter leaves. Afterward it no longer seemed to matter. "Like a rainbow for crows," she said. "A redbird in a world of kites." Antlike, the dissenters hurried across the cold landscape in their serious leaf colors, swarming together on the Sabbath, busily moving between pens and barn and house.

She closed her eyes. Mr. Taylor was speaking again, looking acutely into the fire as though he might find a small, tormented creature writhing in the flames, but Cath no longer listened.

"Gabriel," she murmured. How much longer before Goodman Cook reached Albany, swaying on his rickety mare? Then a trip west, a journey east. But she could wait, knew well how to wait.

When Mr. Taylor's voice rose, Catherwood opened her eyes.

"Before the flood, angels mated with the

daughters of men. Do you believe that? Do you believe every word from heaven?"

"Ah, you be angry at me now."

Cath looked down at her stitching, bit her thread in two. She could hear the babe James screaming, could hear Sam stomping up and down in the next room. Now that the risk of contagion was past, Sarah Dumbleton and Sam shared her room. When she had climbed into bed the night before, a grease lamp sputtered on the chair and Sam already slept, his arms thrown carelessly out and his blond hair flung in a halo around his head. His mouth hung ajar, a single drop of moisture on his cheek, and his milk teeth shone, each intact and in its place. Hard to believe such a cherub would grow gravemouthed like his father, hair darkening, teeth rotten stumps to be grubbed out of his jaw. Yet there was a sweetness in Mr. Taylor, a tenderness to his wife and sons. Old Testament honey from the lion's carcass. Perhaps a sleeping childhood shone inside the raven.

"Children of angels, Mr. Taylor? Angels and archangels," she said, "and all the company of heaven."

* * *

Cath rummaged in her pack, ousting a red squirrel who raced away chittering, fishing out her boots and the trapper's moccasins, placing her slippers on top. She would have to be back at the minister's house before nightfall, but now for a few hours she was free of labor and walls. She followed the frozen river north, her stride lengthening and cloak flapping behind. Under ice the water piped its persistent spring song as Cath jumped from stone to stone, slipping on rime. The trapper's pack felt light—a basket of air—and she raced through the bare trees, branches snagging her cloak, the bough of an evergreen slapping her face. A mild sun lit the woods, touching the leaf-blocked dens of animals, the leaves and red berries of wintergreen Catherwood picked from the forest floor. Impulsively she clambered over stones and reached the ice. Now she could travel swiftly, the dusting of snow not hindering her steps. A mile north of the village she built a fire and cooked a chine piece of venison with a sliced garden skirret. After days of rye bread, pease porridge, and vegetables boiled to a pulp, the meat smelled fragrant. "Bestest," Catherwood said, spearing the venison with her knife.

Her portion of the deer brought to the Taylor door was sweeter here, under a sky packed with snow clouds. There was no anxious fretting here, no rooms so narrow that she could not be alone in her thoughts.

Manners! A-borned in the dish kettle and a-breed up in a turf heap.

Cath gave out the glimmer of a smile, remembering Henry Pasturel's description of Albany traders. She liked to think of Mr. Taylor as a whimsical mix of good and ill, but at last he had made her angry, talking of his own birth.

"Born a victor in the chronicles of Christ," he said, "born during the battle of Edgehill, bristling just a few miles off in Sketchley. A paradise birth, as Cavaliers were tossed here and there, dashed and broken on the ground."

"My mother's husband died at Edgehill," Cath said. "He died very bravely."

"A joyous day," he said, "when we Christian English overtopped the swords and battlements of kings."

Deaf as a haddock. Deaf to any who were not dissenters. Yet in the end the bodies of Cromwell and Bradshaw and Ireton were forced from their tombs among the kings and queens, and strung up at Tyburn gallows. Or so they had heard in Somerset.

Catherwood walked faster, almost jumping into a run, kicking her patched smock and gown. She spoke to Mr. Taylor angrily, imagined he sat still to hear about her twisted path through the forest and hills, to hear that she had fasted months in the wilderness without the comfort of walls and ceiling. That she could not be fettered by his constraints, that she sailed upward into the sun as he tried to seize her wings, pin her to his specimen board. No Christian child, she told him, simmers and shrieks in a fiery lake. Not this one that goes along with me like a shadow child, nor any other. Nor his child. She remembered a pretty picture from one of his sermons—the sea of God as a quilt ball in a silver box. Hers was no toy sea but a bottomless spirited swell that reared up, ballasting home and husband, a whole ark of affections. Her sea rolled turbulent with ebbs and flood like the sea Taylor had crossed from Wapping-upon-Thames to Boston harbor, with sullen calms and storms when the waters flashed above his ship. He had described sunfish to her, suspended on top of the water by the sun's force—he had seen hoarse-voiced whales "blothering" in waves, a red spark like a bumblebee zig-zagging above the twilit surface of sea. She meant to tell him that the whole sea was lured by the tide, though each creature floated and swerved. Likewise was the fluent flying of souls through the vast sea of God, all their lives a continual passage. And there were many roads through wilderness, many paths to the city. The things she wanted to tell him! But he was the clergyman, she a woman, uncovenanted, without friends in his village.

And yet, here in the forest, she forgave the man his vanity, his narrow rule over the town.

"But I will not bide," she whispered. "Give me bait for the journey, compass, and map in spring, or those things with a horse in winter, and I will not bide."

That much she had told him face-to-face after Tithingman Cornish came to question her. Though it was not true, she thought now; she must remain and bear the dissenters and the passing of months, even if waiting was a weary work.

"These trapper- and farmer-saints," she

said aloud, "be a serious altogether strange people."

Such odd events she had witnessed in Westfield. Mr. Taylor christened an infant, Hannah Sacket, with a chunk of blue ice, rubbing it on the child's skull until the baby shrieked and meltwater made runnels down her face. The meetingplace itself seemed unchurchly, half powder magazine and half meetinghouse, with the minister in his tub pulpit above the people, the elders facing outward, men and women divided on hard backless benches, dwindling in age and rank as they moved away from the pulpit. Then morning and afternoon sermons, the chattering of teeth all that Catherwood could hear after an hour passed, then the slow mechanical stamping of stiff feet, louder and louder until the raven lifted his wings and bade them cease. A voice, Dewey or Ashly or Whiting or Granger, a man's or a woman's but unreal like the cry of an injured bird: *How shall I be saved?* Now and then the minister's rich or homespun words snared Cath's attention, although she shut her mind against the words that promised sweetness to his own elect but the endless lake of fire to Elisabeth. His people stood to stare down

God and pray, wrestling in words. Last came the terrible singing, to Cath a fierce joyless noise that would scare the wilderness.

Cath threaded in and out the woods around Westfield, the only soul in the village who was not always occupied. Mrs. Taylor had told her that November was the month for weddings, but she glimpsed no bride-ale, no sign of celebration in the streets or meetinghouse. Once, an hour before sunset, she had seen a knot of people dump the rude coffin of a child into the ground. No black token of ribbon or glove or scarf showed their sorrow, but later, as dark gathered, the mourners spilled out into the graveyard. Even the smallest children were drunk; they reeled and lost footing on the slick ground. A man carrying an infant toppled in the open grave and had to be dragged out again. Cath was glad to hear the baby's screams; at least it lived. Later she looked in the grave and saw the butt ends of several child-sized coffins projecting into the hole. Here and there in the burying ground a paling or granite lump marked a grave.

In the forest she returned to a world less muddy, more beautiful. She felt free to remember in the woods, unconstrained by the intensity of Mr. Taylor's people. "Perhaps I be wrong," she said, "and they'm not afraid." But if her fear for Elisabeth had seemed hands at her throat, then these sin-alarmed people were gripped, possessed by fear. There was Mrs. Taylor, fainting in the hall because the Devil growled *You killing me* in the voice of her son Sam. Mrs. Dumbleton claimed to have seen the shoulder blades of a red heifer lengthen out and turn to bony plates that bore her clanking above the trees. The whole town hated the darkness lurking in the woods, scanned the star-speckled sky for portents, and seemed to dread Cath because she survived the blackness of trees and night—and Tithingman Cornish had reproved her for nightwalking, warning her to stay within doors after the hour of candle-lighting.

The last of her own fear of the forest had fallen away after Elisabeth died. She no longer wanted to snip and shape the woods to the pattern of an English garden. *Brimmle and brushet be best.* They were a better refuge as they grew, wild flourishing temples. Cath's hand grazed the package of bones. She remembered the chapel in the woods near their house, how when she had stepped to the altar rail her unborn baby leaped in the womb as if for joy. No, the forest was not evil, although crooked and lacking the comforts of houses. Lost in trees and open meadows, she had gone on living, delighted in her child, found reason enough to praise the God whose ways were past understanding. Pictures were stamped in her memory: Elisabeth tottering through a meadow of bee balm or splashing in a shallow pool floored with pebbles. Even longing for home and husband, Catherwood had known moments when the spring air wove crowns around her head, when the sunlight seemed to arrow through her body.

"No," she said. "There may be much good in these dissenters, but the world and God be better than they dream. And to kneel on the skin of the world is meet, not to glare God down and batter Him with argument."

She scoured the skillet with dirt and sand, then tucked it deep in her pack.

"So cold, Elisabeth," she said, "too cold to bide. And cock-light soon."

For a few minutes she lingered, shut her eyes, and tried to imagine herself with Gabriel. If she returned safely home, if home held secure, they would bury Elisabeth when their traveling clergyman visited in the spring. And poor little Fan would marry Richard, if Sarah, weakened from childbirth, had died over the winter. Or Robert, if Mary had died. Elisabeth's bones would rest in blessed ground, near enough to visit. *Minimy pinimy, where is she?* At home she could tell her sorrow, name her grief in ceremony, show it in black cloak and ribbons. Already both Elisabeth and Gabriel were less distinct in memory. Cath pictured each in fragments, hair, color of eyes and lashes, turn of a jaw or nose. Strange to lose Elisabeth's face, when Cath still woke feeling a child's warmth on her skin, curls against her cheek.

"Elisabeth. The world upside down, gone ban twivy twist, Elisabeth. And Gabriel."

Her sense of him had faded among the dissenters. Tall, he was tall, would tower over short Mr. Taylor. The hair was black, so black that she was surprised Elisabeth could shine so fair, so much like herself as a child. She imagined Gabriel's naked skin, pale against the indigo coverlet Lacey had given them. Like a white flame in the dusk. Then the eyes, the first thing she had noticed about him, a startling blue against the whiteness of skin and the black of his hair. His voice, like all those from Somerset, appeared beautiful in memory, far different from the nasal tones of the dissenters. And his speech was educated, refined by academy and Oxford but not showy and over-decorated with coinings and long words. She and Gabriel worked hard like these people, but their lives were more peaceful, less a wrestle with ill angels.

Some day or month soon she would go, and whether she journeyed to York or even afterward to Virginia or back to Somerset, this frontier town would diminish in her thoughts.

"Nothing left but a raven and a whirl of leaf fall."

Day by day she grew more eager to leave. She wondered whether Gabriel would send Henry or James or Will or would come himself. Even in imagination she felt a disappointment, thinking that he might not travel such a long way in winter. She felt almost as though Gabriel's failure to dare the wilderness for her sake would be such a stroke that she could not love him so much as before. She pictured the arrival a hundred times, and once it would be Henry, the next time Will or James. But perhaps the men would stay at home, and Gabriel would trail Goodman Cook through the snow and hills. Or ride alone, secure with map and compass. It would be a hard passage to Westfield and back again, for although the snows were still moderate, any week might come the heavy falls so common at the turn of the year, so difficult for a man or a horse. *Gabriel.* He might arrive at night while she slept, and there would be a rustling through the town as he was pointed to Mr. Taylor's fortified house. The horses might reach Westfield as she did, in the midst of psalm-singing, or at candle-teeming when the meetinghouse bell tolled. When she pictured him walking toward her, Catherwood knew a sharp and naked feeling, like the gasp in a room when a sword flashes from its scabbard. She remembered the little wilderness planted by Grevel House, and the day her hand first rested in Gabriel's hand, with her sleeve laid upon his sleeve as they walked in the garden.

"Gabriel," she called, sweeping up her patched gown and racing along the frozen river.

Abruptly Catherwood stopped to listen,

furling the cloak with its bones around her body. Fine as spider's floss, echoes of *Gabriel* floated through the trees. *Not this day. But soon.* Once again she could feel the raveled thread between them, as though the silken twist were being reeled back, tensing in her grip.

Gabriel. She imagined his eyes, his hands, the strong legs. His face, winter-pale, refined by grief: would there be a tightening around the mouth, an expression in his eyes, some small telltale sign as he approached? And of what? The months when he knew her dead but hoped and often believed she lived. The certainty that she cradled no child in her arms. That he glimpsed her altered face, saw in it a change more or less beautiful, surely more grave, surely older and more enduring, the face given her by God and wilderness.

Epilogue

[Copied into the Church Record, Westfield, the colony of Massachusetts in New-England, on the first of December Anno Domini 1678.]

A remarkable instance of Gods Providence fell out among us on a Sabbath in the tenth month, being the sudden wondrous apearance after second sermon and psalm of a fair girl, bedotcht with dirt but dresst in tatters that did speak finely of ranck and elegance and that she was not one of our kind. Whereupon our scared people did crye out against her as mad, so that she, seeming bewildered, did protest her innocence, that she was not mazed but lost, as a Lamb in the wilderness: and an elder did say, "This Sabbath we are made the ninety and nine and she the one lost." Yet though she did stay with us some fortie nights and dayes, eating and sleeping in our houses, attending our worship, we still knew nothing of her, she being secretive and tazzled in her mind, trouble harrowing up her feelings; for she wandered many monthes in snick-snarls of forests, perhaps north toward the French collonies. One of our own people vollunteered with a compass to go west of the Hudson, where none from this place travelled before, a place famous for Unicornes and strange beasts, &c., to search out her people, she promising a fine reward. This man returned home againe with golde Angells and with the prize of a bay horse, everie inch neat made and useful. And he met with Unicornes, pearly with gliddering horns, that when they glimpst him peeking, nayed and changed shape to children and skipt laughing into the selvedge of woods.

Toward the close of the eleventh month and during a light snowfall, one did come after Mistress Catherwood: being a Horseman, and dresst in velvet doublet and breeches of the deep rich black fit onlie for a great churchman or governour, belted with a sword, and with costlie lace spilling from beneath his velvet cloak: his face serious and handsome to look on, white and unmarked in complexion with blue eyes and thick black hair loose to his shoulders, cut straight and low on his brows. Being such a noble sight riding a fine bay horse and leading another that we English, who are not loathe to greet a stranger, drew back in silence, one sassie fellow onlie calling after his name. Some heard "Gabriell" and others the word "Light," so that some thought to see the Angell with blasing sword in hand at Edens Garden, others the high ArchAngel, whose name we darsn't lend to mortal child.

Coming behind him to the place where the woman stayd, we saw her walking up and down in the snowie field behind the house as was sometime her custom, and all watched her turn toward the horseman, but with no change of face but the same settled quiet and sadness, only lifting her armes a little outward in misterious gesture, for she never among us smiled: and in a twinckling this Gabriel did flash down upon her and raise her up to the horse, riding on without stopping so that in an instant they flew into a popple grove and vanished utterlie, even the stamped marks of hooves drifting up with snow.

The people did stand thunder stricken and uneasie with raw notions, looking one on the other, but after onlie a few minites the horses flowd back out of the trees, Mistress Catherwood and the stranger still riding the one mare, and she dresst in a fair black cloak and holding her ragged cloak bundled in her arms. His hand proved strong and seeming mortel, and the man and the woman did stay among our people for three nights, the man generous with thanks and with gold.